Misery Mess and Miracles

Angela E Stevenson

Disclaimer

This book is based on some true events, however, has been fictionalized and all persons appearing in this work are fictitious. Any resemblance to real people, living or dead is entirely coincidental.

Please visit our website for contact information

www.miserymess-miracles.com

ISBN-13: 978-0615614236 (Alegna Media Publishing, LLC)
ISBN-10: 061561423X

DEDICATION

To my beloved mother, Mrs. Elizabeth Sheppard, I love and miss you dearly. I am so grateful to have had you as my mother. I am who I am as a woman because of the values you taught me. May you rest in peace.

To my Father, thanks for being who you are. I've learned a lot from you throughout my years of life. All is well and I love you.

Lastly, but not least I dedicate this book to my two wonderful Grandchildren;
Jamiah Hampton & Kaine Stevenson, Nana loves you guys so much and I pray many blessings, love and success upon your life.

ACKNOWLEDGMENTS

First and foremost I give honor to God from whom all blessings flow. I never could have accomplished anything without the help of Almighty God. I'm so grateful to know who God is and most importantly that he knows who I am.

To my children, Ty, Jamekas, Javaris and Ezekiel, thanks for your continued support and love; you guys have been my rock and have helped me remain strong even when you're getting on my nerves. (lol) I love you guys forever and a day. Candace Mason Ryan thanks for your encouraging words and your faith to believe that I could finish the work. To Melissa Washington who has always been one of my biggest fans; thanks also for keeping all my original work because it came in handy when my computer crashed. Danita Draughn thanks for re-proofing my book, you aren't just a reader but a proof-reader too! I truly appreciated your help. To my sister, Patricia Goins, you have given me inspiration through your own tenacity to pursue your dreams regardless of the obstacles that has come your way. I can't forget to mention my Godparents, Suffr.Bishop Reuben & First Lady Graham, you know I love you guys beyond what words can express! You guys have loved me through my worst, I appreciate the prayers, chastisement and encouragements; your seeds were sown on good ground. Special acknowledgments to the Sheppard, Goins, Johnson, Young, Anderson, Gees &Smith families, Thank you for your individual contributions in my life, we're connected for life and I love you guys always! To all other friends and loved ones that I could not call by name, thanks for being who you are in my life, you are appreciated. Lastly and least, to the devil himself and all the people you used to wreak hell in my life, You thought you were going to kill me and shut me up but I survived, so guess what? You lose but I WIN!!!

Misery

I can't believe I did this again! I promised myself that I wouldn't have sex again until I was married, not to mention having sex with this don't have time for a relationship; see you only when I have time man. But darn the sex is the bomb diggity!
Harvey really knew how to put it to a sista'. From the very first time we made love I was addicted to Harvey's eye-glass wearing self. The way he looked at me made my juices start to flow. The soft touch of his fingers as they caressed my body ignited my fire. Ooh! The man had major skills when it came down to using his juicy brown lips.

He would start at my ears and blow gently into my ears. His cool breath lingered in my ears as he created a trail to my neck. He licked and sucked as if he were eating a cherry-flavored lolli-pop. It didn't take long for him to have me at the point of no return. His tongue was the paint brush and my body was his canvas. And he definitely was very skilled in his techniques; he had mastered the art of seduction.

Harvey always seemed to take delight in pleasing me; he did whatever it took to make sure I was satisfied in every way. He knew all the right places to linger and how to work each part of me. It was always my pleasure to be with Harvey because he would always take me to ecstasy. He would have me calling on Jesus and speaking in an unknown tongue.

Shoot! Let me stop laying here thinking about what he does to me before I have to roll over and go for a third round. God knows he'd be willing but there is no time for that, it's almost 5:30 am and I have to have him out of my house before the kids wake up.

I sneak him in and sneak him out because I don't want my four children Mynesha, Jamiria, and twins La'nyse and Ja'nyse to know that I get my groove on. They would have a fit if they knew I had some man in my room. They think that since I'm a youth leader at St. Johns Holiness Church and because my parents happen to be Pastor Leroy and First Lady Inez Shelton that my life has no fun or excitement unless it involves the church. Humph! Little do they know! Therefore, I must maintain my innocent and holy image not only for their sake but for my parent's also. Plus, I didn't want to deal with the embarrassment and humiliation of the church if they knew that I wasn't as holy as everyone else. No one could ever know that the first family is less than perfect: daddy would never have that.

It's not that often that Harvey gets to come by because of his hectic schedule as a twenty-four hour maintenance man. Sometimes, I wonder just how much or what kind of maintenance he is really doing? But he swears he loves me and I believe him; but I sometimes hate the fact that his business keeps him from making a true commitment to me. It has been two years now and he still is saying that as soon as he gets established enough then he'll think about getting married but, for right now we're just going with the flow and enjoying each other's company. It didn't matter because I knew I had his heart even without the commitment.

"Hey, Yolanda baby, you up already?" Harvey asks in a groggy voice. "Yes, boo I'm up and you better get up too. It's almost 6 o'clock and the kids will be waking up soon." Harvey rolls out of bed but not before wrapping his arms around me and pulling me towards him. He holds me tight as if he hated to let me go. We relax in each other's arms for a moment as unspoken words are exchanged between us. Words didn't have to be uttered because our love spoke for itself. That's how in sync we were. Finally we reluctantly release each other because time waits for no man.

As Harvey is getting dressed disappointment hurriedly set in. Not because he has to leave but because he takes a part of me with him every time he leaves. Also because I know fornication is wrong; I've been taught that all my life. *'The wages of sin is death, but the gift of God is eternal life.* That's what my father used to say every Sunday from the pulpit. So every time I sleep with Harvey I condemn myself to hell! But I couldn't stop no matter how hard I tried; deep down I didn't want too. I loved that man.

As much as I wanted to quit sleeping around I couldn't. Heck! What's a sista to do? I still consider myself young at the ripe age of 35. My 5'6 mocha brown complexion; size 12 medium built frame attracts the younger men, middle aged and the older men; from the beggar man to the rich man; I've been told that my beautiful smile that is encompassed with dimples is my feature attraction. And once they get to know my winning personality mixed with my warm character, it's all over. That's not being conceited that is just the pure facts. So what am I to do when TAAD *(tall, attractive and dark*) comes my way? My body still craves love and attention. Just because my ex chose to run off doesn't mean that my hormones did too!

I kiss Harvey good-bye and watch as his 6"3 dark chocolate statue walks to his car. I contently watch his defined profile as he drives away, wondering when I'll see him again? But at the same time I'm beating myself up as I make my way back to the place where we made passionate love. I ask God's forgiveness for the umpteenth time and vow not to do it again; knowing goodness well that if he shows up tomorrow that back in his sculptured arms I'll be. Doggone it! I'm tired of fighting what I really feel and I'm tired of sneaking around for fear of what someone else may think of me or because I'm trying to protect everyone else. But every since I was a child that's what I've learned to do. Hide the truth.

My childhood was very sheltered. Being a PK's (Preachers kid) I was limited in the things I could do. Basically, I could go to school; I could go to church and I could watch cartoons. Anything else beyond that was a rarity.

I rarely got to spend the night over anyone's house other than family but even that was seldom. Daddy was too scared someone was going to corrupt my mind. Momma didn't have much of a say so because whatever daddy said was the law.

I was not an only child but I felt like it. I had been a foster child that the Shelton's took in when I was six months old. Years later they adopted me when I was twelve years old. My mother Inez never had any birth children of her own. She married into a readymade family but she still desired to have a child that she could call her own.

Therefore, my dad agreed to adopt another child. It was my mother's choice to adopt a little girl. They never hid the fact that I was adopted and they told me that they didn't know my birth parents either. No one ever made it a big deal that I was adopted I was treated as a normal part of the family. I guess I was the only one that really had problems with it but I kept that to myself. I didn't want to seem ungrateful.

My daddy had previously been married and had three other children. Darissa, Anthony and Timothy were much older and had already left home by the time I came along with the exception of Darissa. She left and went to college and later moved to Detroit after graduating. She later moved back home for a while before she left and moved in with her boyfriend. But what do a twenty-five year old and a ten-year old have in common, nothing except that we have the same daddy.

Even though there was a huge age gap between us Darissa would take me along with her on some of her outings. I enjoyed going to the mall and the movies and visits over to some of her friend's house. She was the one person who let me be myself. I remember wishing that I were grown like her. She had freedom to come and go as she pleased. She defied mostly everything daddy said. *"You can't make me go to church if I don't want to go"* She'd scream. And daddy would yell his favorite scripture, "The wages of sin is death and the gift of God is eternal life. You will never have eternal life living in sin." Or he would say, *"As for me and my house we will serve the Lord!"* *"But it didn't say I had to serve him today,"* she'd shout back. I found it funny and interesting that he could never make Darissa follow his rules. She simply stood her ground and did what she wanted to do.

Darissa didn't seem to care. She would say she went to church enough when she was younger to last her a lifetime. I certainly understood that. Daddy pretty much considered her a lost case. But often times he'd say, *"I raised her right and she'll return to her proper upbringing one day."* As far as I could see that day was never coming. Darissa went to clubs and parties and would come home in the wee hours of the morning. I couldn't wait to be grown so that I could be just like Darissa. I always felt safe when she was around too.

Sadly, to say I don't have a lot of good memories of my childhood. Like most adults today can sit and tell you all of their wonderful childlike adventures, I can't. I have bits and pieces of memories some good and a lot bad. I remember playing alone in the back yard of our modest split-level home in Cleveland, Ohio. In school I was often picked on as a child because they said I had big eyes and because I wore old-fashioned clothes.

Even though the kids sometimes picked on me I still managed to get in trouble where the boys were concerned. I remember in kindergarten my mother was called to the school because this little boy and I were caught in the closet. I had my pants down and was trying to pull his down too. My mother was appalled because she was the preacher's wife and her child exhibited such bad behavior. *"I'm so sorry Mrs. Carter; I don't know where she learned such filth. Probably from some of her older cousins,"* my mother embarrassingly said. My teacher Mrs. Carter quickly agreed.

I was fussed at all the way home. All I heard was how upset she was and how embarrassing it would be if the church ever heard about it. She never once asked me why I did it or where I learned it from. After getting my butt whipped with three switches braided together I was sent to my room. I overheard my mother tell daddy." *You never know what is in her bloodline. It's a risk you take when you take in an orphan child."* I remember asking myself what she meant by that. It had to be something bad because my father angrily replied, *"That is why I didn't want to get her anyway. I knew it would cause problems in the long run. And here she is five years old and she already being fast!"* But I couldn't have been too fast since I got caught!

When I was ten years old I got in trouble again because I let this boy named Gary walk me home. He had written me a note in our reading class that read, *'will you go with me? Yes or no.'* I circled yes! Although I didn't know where we were going, I was just happy that he wanted me to go. After class I asked him," *Where do you want me to go?" I can go but I can't be late getting home, ok."* I thought maybe he wanted me to go to the corner store during lunchtime or at recess time. A lot of the kids would sneak and walk to the store during that time. Little did I know that was not what he wanted.

In between laughs he told me, *"No! Silly, I mean will you be my girl. You know, go steady."* I really didn't know but since he better explained it, my answer was still yes! He told me that since we were girlfriend and boyfriend he was supposed to walk me home. Since I only lived two blocks from the school I didn't see any harm in that. So after school he met me outside by the swings and we walked the two blocks in silence.

I don't know why he was quiet but I was quiet because I didn't know what to say. He was my first boyfriend, so maybe we weren't supposed to talk. All I know was that I was excited a boy was walking me home.
When we got to my house we walked up on the porch and before I knew it he kissed me! His black crusty lips touched mine. He didn't even give me a chance to close my eyes. I did know you were supposed to close your eyes because Laura closed her eyes when Luke kissed her on General Hospital. General Hospital was my mother's favorite soap opera and it was always on when I got home from school.

"Did you like it?" he asked while smiling. "Yes" I said with my head hung down. He then asked me did I want to do it again and of course I said yes. But this time I told him let me close my eyes. He did. I wet my lips so that his lips wouldn't feel so dry upon mine and I closed my eyes and puckered my lips. He slowly leaned forward and kissed me again. Before we could complete the kiss I heard my mother yell, *"What in the name of God are you doing? Get your fast self in this house!"* I was thinking, *'I don't know why they keep calling me fast when it seems I am slow because I keep getting caught!"*

I quickly opened my eyes and jumped back. Gary made a beeline off the porch and down our driveway. My mother snatched me into the house and commenced to slapping me all upside the head. She didn't bother getting the switches like she usually did. *"Why are you letting some boy kiss on you? You know better than that!"* she hollered at me while slapping me on the left side of my head. I really didn't know better, but I certainly knew now!

When my dad came home my mother told him how she caught me kissing some little boy. He came in my room and preached to me about all sinners going to hell. *"For the wages of sin is death."* He repeated for the thousandth time. Yea, yea I heard it all before I thought to myself. Everything I do is a sin, what can I do that isn't a sin I wondered to myself. But if kissing Gary was a sin then too bad because I was already thinking of a way to do it again. Maybe it isn't a sin if you don't get caught. I think it was at this time that I began to develop my rebellious ways.

Later that night I overheard my parents having another conversation about me." *We have trouble on our hands. She is probably acting just like her mother,"* My father said. But how did he know since he didn't even know who she was?

When I turned 13 years old we moved from Ohio to a small city called Lafayette, Georgia. As a teenager I was not allowed to play sports or go to the many school parties my school had. If I asked to go to any school function it would start a major lecture from my parents. My momma would ask in her level toned voice, *"Why would you ask such a thing when you already know the answer?"* Then my daddy would follow up with, *"We are servants of the Lord and what would the church think if I let my child go to these devilish parties? We can't preach one thing and let our child do another."* Then he'd go on and on about how he made mistakes with his other children but he promised he wouldn't make the same mistakes with me. I guess he meant that my brothers and sister weren't raised completely in the church because he had only been preaching for seventeen years and pastoring for the last eight years.

Since I didn't have any leisure activities outside of church, singing became my favorite thing to do. I would sing in church and at home. Everybody would rant and rave about my singing abilities. I would have to sneak and listen to the radio in order to hear secular music. My parents called it the devils music. I used to dream about becoming a well-known singer. I enjoyed all types of music. I wanted to sing and it didn't matter the type of music gospel or R&B. Since I was in church all the time, gospel is what I sang the most.

Besides school and church I really didn't have much of a life. Living in the south however did bring new meaning to my life. It was in Lafayette that I fell in love for the first time. I met a girl named Honey that lived across the street from me. Honey was a couple years older than me but we hung out from time to time. My parents didn't mind me hanging with Honey because she was a homey looking type of girl. The typical 'girl next door' type that never got into trouble. My parents felt she would be good for me.

One summer evening Honey asked me to go with her to help her take some braids out of one of her friends head. I agreed to go. We walked down the street to her friend's house and upon walking through the door I received the surprise of my life.

Standing at the door was a tall, dark skinned, medium built handsome man. He had thick eyebrows that met in the middle above his hazel eyes. A thin mustache trimmed the top of his thick lips. And to my surprise his head was lined with thin cornrows. Is this the person Honey was talking about? Yes, indeed it was.

"Hey girl, I thought you weren't coming. What took so long? He asked her in a deep baritone voice. I was immediately attracted to him. *"I had to finish washing the*

dishes first and then I went and got Yolanda," She replied back.

He turned to me and looked directly into my eyes and said, *"Hi Yolanda, what's up?"* All I could say was," *Hi."* Honey introduced him as Tyler. Tyler Davis.

We went into Tyler's room and Honey began to take down the braids in his head. I sat in a nearby chair and watched and listened to their conversation. They basically talked about their families and other people in the neighborhood.

In Lafayette where we lived it was rural and family oriented. Everyone in our neighborhood knew everybody. So Tyler already knew that I was the preacher's kid from Ohio with the proper accent. Our family was respected and well liked because of my dad's position as a pastor.

Tyler asked, *"How do you like it here in Lafayette, Yolanda?"* Oh my goodness I thought, he said something to me! I was filled with delight. *"I like it ok."* I responded while looking around his dimly lit room. I couldn't look him in the eyes for fear he could tell that I liked him. About forty-five minutes later and only half way finished with unbraiding Tyler's hair; Honey announces that she's tired and has to leave. *"Tyler, I'm tired it's taking too long to take your hair down. Can I finish tomorrow?"* She says

in an annoying tone. Dang! I'm not ready to go yet. I think to myself. *"Honey, you can't leave my hair like this. I'm going out tonight"*. He quickly replies while trying to turn to look at her. I wanted to ask where he was going, but it didn't matter it wasn't like I could go anyway.
Honey looks at me and asks, *"Yolanda, can you finish this up for me, because I'm tired?"* I knew I should have said no because my mother didn't know where I was and it was already dusk dark outside. I was supposed to be in the house before dark, which meant I needed to be on my way home now. However, I couldn't say no. I didn't want to leave him with a mini Afro on one side and raggedy looking braids on the other side. *"Yea, I'll finish it for you."* I said. No sooner than I had said yea she handed me the comb that she'd been using to comb out the braids. She told Tyler bye and I told him I'd be right back so I could walk her to the door.

When I came back into the room, he told me thank you. I continued taking the braids out of his head while listening to some old school music on the radio. It only took about another thirty minutes to finish taking the braids out. While finishing his hair his brother Tyrell came home. Tyler introduced me and told him that Honey left me there to finish his hair. They laughed and Tyrell said, *"Nice meeting you."* Then left and went to his room but not before doing a quick inspection of me from head to toe.

While I was combing out his braids we talked and laughed as if we were old friends. He told me his plans of going into the Army and I told him of my dream of becoming a famous singer. I shouldn't have told him I like to sing because he asked me to sing him something. I only knew church songs so I sung a stanza of *'Amazing Grace'* He told me that I did have a nice voice and that he hoped I would become famous one day. You should have seen the huge smile I had on my face; someone believed in me.

"I'm on the last braid." I say to Tyler as I comb out the kinks in his hair. I was actually glad that this was the last braid because my arms had started to get tired. Instead of Tyler saying thank you, he reached up and grabbed my hand and pulled me around to sit on his lap. When I sat on his lap he kissed me! My heart fell to my stomach. It was totally unexpected. I didn't know what to do, so I kissed him back. Other than Gary back in grade school this was my first real kiss. I tasted beer as he wedged his tongue inside my mouth. I really didn't know how to kiss but I guess I was doing ok because he kept on kissing me. He even picked me up and laid me on his bed, which was just a step away from the wooden chair that we were sitting in.

After laying me on the bed he laid on the side of me and looked at me as if looking at me for the first time. I hoped that my white jeans and red and white-checkered top didn't look too childish. *"You're beautiful, you know that right."* He said while looking down at me. No one had ever told me that I was beautiful. I was told by adults, that I was a cute little girl, but no one had ever told me I was beautiful. To me beautiful was far better than being cute. Anybody could be cute. Babies are cute when they are first born; you're cute when you say your Easter speech; a puppy is cute. But to be called beautiful is something special. And at that very moment for the first time in my life I felt special. I simply replied by saying, *"Thank you!"*

It was way past my time to be at home and I'm sure that my mother was wondering where I was. I figured I was going to be in big trouble when I got home but at this time I didn't care. I was in the arms of a man that said I was *beautiful*. I wonder did he know I was only thirteen years old. I heard him tell honey that he would be twenty years old in July. So that made him nineteen years old. I guess age didn't matter to him or maybe I acted so mature that he didn't think about our ages.

We rolled around on the bed and kissed and hugged until he tried to unbutton my pants. I told him to stop; not because I really wanted him too but because I knew I had to get home. I didn't want to show my real age by saying I had a curfew, so I told him I had to leave because my mom and I had somewhere to go.

"I hate you have to leave. Hopefully, I can see you again." He said while pulling me up off the bed. *"Ok!"* I said. I didn't know what else to say. I was still in awe about what had just happened. He gave me his number and told me to call anytime. I couldn't give him my phone number because I couldn't receive phone calls from boys. One time I was paired with a boy in my science class to work on a school project. He happened to call one evening and mom answered the phone. She hit the roof! *"Yolanda doesn't receive phone calls from boys,"* she firmly stated. I came running into the kitchen to explain why I gave him the number. I was embarrassed, I can only imagine how the boy felt. Therefore, I took Tyler's number without offering mine and he didn't ask for it either. He walked me to the door and kissed me goodnight.

As I walked home I was thinking of a lie to tell my mother when she asked me where I was. It was almost 9:00p.m so I just knew I was in for it. When I walked in the house she was on the phone talking to her best friend that lived down the street. I went straight to my room. About thirty minutes later I hear her call my name."Yolanda!" she yelled from the kitchen.

"Maam" I hollered back while walking towards the kitchen. I knew she was going to say come here. *"Yes, maam, what is it?"* I said as I reached the kitchen. She had this stern look on her face. *"Where were you and Honey at all this time"*, she asked. I didn't know whether to lie or tell the truth, so I told half the truth. *"We went down the street to help one of her friends take her braids out of her hair."* I quickly lied. Well it wasn't all a lie. We did help a friend take down braids but the friend happened to be a he instead of a she. And I would never tell her that Honey left me there by myself. She continued to look at me with frustration in her eyes. *"The next time you want to go somewhere other than Honey's house you need to come and ask me first! I thought you were still down Honey's house, but when I called, her mother said you all weren't there. She didn't know where you guys were at either."* I hurriedly replied, *"Yes maam"* while trying to sound sorrowful. *"Now go on and make sure you have your clothes laid out for church tomorrow"* she said as I walked back towards my room. I didn't bother to respond this time. I was just glad that she didn't ask what Honey's friend's name was. I wondered where Honey went when she left Tyler's house. Good thing for me that she wasn't at home when mom called.

Church was boring as usual. My dad was only the assistant pastor at Free Will Church of God. It started out with Mother Carter singing her favorite song." *Jesus Keep me near the cross."* I don't think she knew any other song because she sung that song repeatedly every Sunday. Then we'd all gather around the altar and be lead in prayer by our only deacon, Deacon Williams. Deacon Williams seemed to have his prayer memorized as most of the church members did too." *Dear heavenly father, soon coming King. It's once more and again that we humbly bow before you. We thank you for our uprising this morning because we could have been dead and sleeping in our graves."* He carried on and on until he reached his closing." *Now father if anything we forgot to utter with our mouths please read the contents of our hearts and answer all these prayers in Jesus name. Amen."* I wouldn't have noticed if he prayed something different anyway because my mind was on the events of the night before. I couldn't get it off my mind. However, my attention was soon focused on the service because testimony service was about to begin.

Testimony service was my favorite part of service. That was the part of the service where you could either speak your testimony or you could sing. I always sang mine. My favorite song was *'I love to Praise him!"* It was a mid tempo type song. But I didn't sing it every Sunday.

Sometimes one of the members would request me to sing,*' Precious Lord'*, that song always got the older members to moaning and waving their hands.

If I sang it well enough someone would always get up and do their little holy dance. One time sister Jones fell out in the floor while shouting. I guess the Lord didn't hear her ask,*" Lord take my hand and help me to stand."* I had never seen that happen before. Deacon Williams and one of the ushers just picked her up and laid her on the pew and fanned her back to life. It was so funny to me that it was hard for me to maintain my composure and finish the song.

I later asked my mother what happened to her and she said she was under the anointing. The anointing should have been *under* her to give her some cushion when she hit that floor because she hit it rather hard.
After that daddy would take up the offering and then either he or Pastor Simmons would preach. The preaching usually had me nodding off to sleep. But today I was wide-awake because I was thinking about Tyler and how I could see him again. Before long they were asking everybody to stand for the benediction. I must have been in thought for a long time.

The summer had come and gone and it was now time to go back to school. I had only seen Tyler twice since our first encounter. Once down Honey's house; the second time I snuck over his house to see him. I didn't get to stay long but I stayed long enough to get me a good kiss. I even let him run his hands in places they should not have been; I liked what he was doing. He slid past first base and had landed on second. He whispered in my ear and said he wanted to skip third base and bat a home run. I knew exactly what he meant from listening to some of the girls at school. He wanted to have sex. I had mixed feelings about going all the way with him. I knew that I shouldn't because my dad had always told me never to go all the way with a boy; or *'make him happy'* as my dad called it. The problem was I wanted to make Tyler happy as I had been making my dad happy.

Yeah, my daddy was sexing me up.

When it first started I thought that was what daddies were supposed to do to and with their daughters. Of course at the age of five I didn't know anything about sex. I thought what we did was normal. I guess that is why I was trying to pull that little boy's pants down in kindergarten. I wanted to do to him what my daddy was doing to me.

I'm not exactly sure when the abuse started but I can remember as far back as five years old. At that age I didn't know anything about abuse. My daddy always said that he liked showing me love. So I just thought that my daddy really loved me. It all started with him tickling me but he would let his hand brush over my would-be breasts. I thought that was fun; tickling made me laugh. My mother never said anything when she saw him tickling me. I'm sure she thought it was all innocent. Besides, what harm is there in tickling your own daughter?

Soon his display of love turned into a secret game. He told me that he didn't want anyone to get jealous of his love for me. I was not to tell anyone about our *'love games'* and I was not to make anyone happy but him. *"Not all children get the type of love that I give you. And if anyone found out about all this love, then they might take you away from us",* he once said while feeling me between my legs. I certainly didn't want anyone to take me away from my home. So I promised to keep it a secret.

We began to play these *'love games'* on a regular basis. Mostly it would be either when my mother was gone to the grocery store and left me at home alone with him, or at night when everyone was sleep. One night he came and lay in the bed next to me with only his underwear on. He told me to be real quite while he pulled my panties off. *"I don't want to wake your mother, Ok,* he whispered. I nodded ok. Once he got my panties off he would tell me to open my legs wide. Then he would rub his fingers between my legs until he reached my *'love spot*". That's the place he liked to show me the most love at. He would rub and poke his fingers in my 'love spot' until I said it hurt. When I told him that it hurt he would only ease up but he didn't stop until he had to go to the bathroom.

He would make this low groaning sound and ask," Do you like giving me love? Do you like making me happy? "Yes", I would say while just laying there. I really wanted him to hurry up because I was sleepy. Soon he would let out this big grunt and say*" that was good, baby. I have to go to the bathroom. You can go back to sleep now."* I always wondered why he always had to go the bathroom afterwards. But now I know he had to clean up from ejaculating. I didn't really find out what that meant until I was much older, but he was doing a lot of it.

Our love secrets continued on a regular basis until I was about ten years old. During that time he never did anything more than touching and feeling me up. Sometimes he would make me touch him which I didn't like doing. When I turned ten years old our love game took a different turn. Instead of just using his hands and fingers, he started getting on top of me and gyrating around. He started to also kiss my now budding breasts. I didn't like him being on top of me. He was very heavy and it was uncomfortable. It was around this time that I started to feel that our 'love games' weren't right.

One day while I was outside playing in the back yard he called for me to come into the house. Momma and Darissa were gone to the store. I came inside thinking that it was time for lunch. He said, *"Let's play the love game."* He didn't wait for an answer but gently took me by the hand and led me to his and momma's room. He told me to take off my pants and lay on the bed. *"Do I have to take my panties off too?"* I asked while taking off my pants. He anxiously replied, *"Yes, and hurry up. You don't want your momma and Darissa to catch you, do you?"*

He made it seem like I would get in trouble if we were caught playing the love game. He often reminded me that no one could ever know that we played the love games; if they did then I would be taken away. That was his way of ensuring that I didn't tell anyone. He was constantly reinventing the idea in my head that people were jealous of us and would be mad if they found out. Therefore, I kept playing this little game that I was quickly getting tired of.

I took off my pants and panties and lay on the bed. He had taken off his pants but still had on his underwear. He laid on top of me and started kissing my breasts and moving around on me. Then he balanced his weight to one side while he pulled out his *'love toy'* and put it up against me. Sometimes he would refer to our private parts as 'love toys'. "My love toy and your love toy belong together. That's what makes it so much fun," he'd say while trying to put his *love toy* inside of mine.

I would tell him that it hurt but he'd just keep going. Maybe he didn't hear me from all the groaning he was doing. When I'd try to move from under him he would just hold me down and say," *Be still! You're messing up the game."* Then he let out his big grunt again and while he was grunting it felt like he was peeing on me. Then I felt something running down my legs.

He got up off me and told me to go to the bathroom and clean up. I grabbed up my clothes and went to the bathroom. On the way to the bathroom I was thinking *'why did he pee on me?'* I cleaned myself up and put my clothes back on and went back outside. However, I couldn't stop questioning why he peed on me. I didn't know at the time that it wasn't pee but sperm. After that incident the love game wasn't fun anymore. I didn't know how to tell daddy that I didn't want to play those games anymore.

The love games became fewer during the time Darissa was at home; and I was glad. Both Darissa and I bedrooms were upstairs. I wondered did she like the love games when she and daddy played them, but I was too scared to ask. When he did want to do the love games I would tell him I didn't want to play anymore because it hurt. By this time he would force me by telling me that I was being disobedient and disobedience was a sin. I didn't want to go to hell for being disobedient so I'd relent and play the love game.

By the time I was twelve I almost had to fight to keep him away from me. I didn't care about going to hell anymore. I just knew something about these games didn't seem right. But he'd always tell me that I would go to hell if I didn't obey him. Or threaten me in some other kind of way. He had put the fear of God in me. Anytime he said anything about going to hell or that God would get me if I don't obey; I would quickly just give in to his commands. I was scared of him and of God. Darn! I grew up being scared and fearful.

Since I was growing older and becoming more aware of things he had to change his tactics in order to keep me from telling on him. The adoption had already taken place by this time so he couldn't tell me that I'd be taken away.

He now used an array of techniques to keep me under his control.
He often played on my emotions and told me that my mother would be so hurt if she knew we were playing these games. *"She won't understand because she's never had a child of her own to understand true love between a father and his child,"* he'd persuasively say.

As a child you believe everything that your parents tell you. Why wouldn't you, since they are responsible for your guidance? When I would question him too much about why I couldn't tell momma he'd resort to a story in the bible. This man had me believing that God had sent me to him to be with sexually. He explained how Sarah had given Haggai to Abraham to sleep with because Sarah couldn't have kids.

He didn't want to have a baby with me, but my mother stayed sick a lot and was not able to perform her wifely duties. As a result I was the substitute for sex. I didn't know what to think or believe. I just knew that I was beginning to hate going to bed at night because that was when he made his attacks.

I recall one night my mother had went to church and left me at home to finish my homework. At this time my dad was working a third shift job so he was in his room asleep.

While she was gone he called me to come into his room but I didn't go. I just knew what he wanted. For some reason he didn't get up and come get me, but when my mother got home he told her what happened. He made it seem that I was just being defiant.

My mother asked," Why didn't you go and see what your daddy wanted when he called you?" She had this look on her face as if she couldn't believe I disobeyed him. With my head hung low I tried to answer her, *"Because I was scared he was going to mess with me,"* I mumbled. "Mess with you how?" she asked while looking confused. I answered while still looking down at the floor," *You know….,* just mess with me! The tears began to flow as she told me I knew better than to think that my dad would mess with me like that.. *"You know goodness well that your daddy would never bother you like that! She replied in a firm tone. You should be ashamed of yourself!"*

Well, I wasn't ashamed; I was so hurt that she didn't believe me. I thought maybe I didn't explain it right. I thought she should have questioned me more and ask why I would say something like that about my father. *"The next time your daddy tells you to do something you'd better do it, if you know what's good for you."* She said yanking me by the arm. I thought she was going to whip me but she didn't.

She was the second person that didn't believe me when I tried to tell them about what was going on. When my adoption was about to be finalized we had to go before a judge for him to make the final determination for the adoption.

They talked to my parents by themselves and then talked to me alone also. When he asked was there any reason that I felt that I should not become adopted by the Shelton's, I tried to tell him about the love games.
I said," *No, but I don't like the games my daddy plays sometimes."* The male judge asked what games. I told him that he lies on top of me and tickles me. He didn't question me any further so I figured he understood what I meant. *"I will certainly ask Mr. Shelton about these love games. I'm sure he means no harm,"* the judge replied.

I guess either he didn't believe me or he never asked daddy about what I said, because the adoption was finalized a week later. So if a judge and your own mother won't believe you, who will. I never mentioned another word about the love games. I felt trapped.

When I started Junior high school in Lafayette it was very exciting. I met new people and started to feel alive. No matter what was happening at home, school was my escape. I poured myself into school and the activities that I could participate in during school hours.

I was still excited about Tyler and me. I even mentioned it to one of my friends, although I never told Honey about what happened because I was afraid she'd tell on me. My other friend told me to leave him alone because he had a girlfriend that was a senior over at the high school. I didn't believe her until Cynthia who happened to be Tyler's girlfriend's sister told me about them.

Cynthia told me that her sister Diane was Tyler's girlfriend. She said that he was over their house all the time. I was hurt but I still wanted to be with Tyler. I called Tyler that same day after school and asked him about his girlfriend. *"You don't have anything to worry about, beautiful. Don't let other people ruin what we have,* he said in his nice voice. He never denied it, but when he called me beautiful I was as putty in his hands. He could have told me anything.

I started sneaking out at night to see Tyler. He only lived a few houses down the street from me. When I knew my parents were sleep I'd sneak out the front door and run over to his house. Tyler's mother always worked third shift so we usually had the house to ourselves except when his brother Tyrell was at home; but it didn't matter because he always went to his room. We had tried on numerous occasions to have sex but failed because he said I was too tight and because it always hurt. It also hurt when dad tried but he wouldn't stop when I told him it hurt.

The first time we actually made love was on November 15, it was the day after my fourteenth birthday. We lie on his couch and kissed and hugged until we both got all hot and bothered. He gently picked me up and carried me to his room. I felt like a queen when he would carry me, it was so romantic. He took his time and peeled off my clothes. Then he started at my neck and licked and sucked my neck as if sucking through a straw, but he was gentle.

Passion marks were big things during that time. He would put one on my neck, just low enough to cover up with the collar of my shirt. Tyler did all kinds of things to my body. He actually did some of the same things that dad did but it felt different. I liked it.

It took a few unsuccessful attempts before he was able to successfully enter me. Even when he did it was a little painful but Tyler was very gentle. I guess the Vaseline helped. I'll never forget the song that was playing on the radio that sat on his nightstand. *'It's going to be an all night thing'* by the Mary Jane Girls filled the room along with our moans and groans.

It was a great night for me, regardless of the fact that I was so young to be indulging in such grown up experiences. At the time I wasn't thinking of that. I was happy to be with the man that seemingly wanted to be with me and me with him. I had been exposed to sex way before Tyler. But no one would know the truth for years to come. People would just pre-judge me as being fast and grown.

I didn't know much about having sex. Tyler had to show me how to move my body. I let out a moan because it felt like he was going to push right through me. *"Does it hurt?* He asked in between his own groans. I could only shake my head back and forth to let him know that I was ok. Pleasure and pain mixed together; I had no words to describe how I felt. The feeling inside of me kept building and building. Just when I felt that I couldn't take it anymore, Tyler reached his peak and our love session came to an end as he collapsed on top of me.

We lay there for a few moments as Tyler caught his breath. Afterwards he helped me clean up and rushed me out the door. I didn't want to go home; I wanted to stay there with him. *"I don't want you to get caught over here and get in trouble, beautiful."* He said while opening the screen door for me. It was something about the way he called me beautiful that made me just melt. I actually started to believe that I was beautiful in spite of how I felt sometimes. I reluctantly left and ran back across the street and walked the short piece back to my house, but not before getting one final good-bye kiss.

All the lights were still out at my house so that was a good sign that my parents were still sleep. I eased the door open and listened for any sound or movement inside the house before going in. All I heard was my mother snoring so I knew the coast was clear. I tiptoed to my room and lay down. I glanced at the clock and it was 3:00a.m. I had four hours before I had to get up to go to school.

It took me a moment to go to sleep because I couldn't believe that I'd just had sex with Tyler. While I was recalling the night's events I realized that I hadn't bled like I overheard some of the girls say they did when they first did it. Maybe that was because daddy had already broken me in.

I finally went to sleep and the alarm clock seemed like it went off five minutes after I went to sleep. I got up and went to the bathroom and noticed that I did have a few brownish red spots in the seat of my white cotton panties. I would just throw them in the wash. Momma would just think that I messed up my panties from having my period.

Tyler and I continued to sneak around until I saw him kissing Diane in his car while they were parked in his driveway. I happened to be walking past his house on my way to the corner store. I saw images and movement as I approached his driveway. I wasn't sure that it was him until I walked into the driveway and saw them.

I didn't know what to say. I just stood there and watched them until they realized that I was standing there. I didn't yell or do anything. I fought back the tears as he rolled down his car window. With a guilty look on his face he asked,*" What you need, Yolanda?"* Is that all that he could say to me? No explanation or I'm sorry or anything. He acted as if he barely knew me; like I was just the little girl from across the street.

Diane just sat there with an annoyed look on her face, as if she wanted me to hurry and go away. Before I could react or respond, Tyrell, Tyler's brother came outside. He looked at me and then looked at Tyrell and Diane in the car. I guess from the look on my face he put two and two together. *"Hey, what's up Yolanda? Where you headed too?"* He said while staring me up and down.

I opened my mouth to speak but no words would come out. I just turned and ran towards the store. My heart felt like it had been shattered into a million pieces. I thought he loved me like I loved him. He had never said it, but why would he make love too me if he didn't love me?

Tyrell reached me before I arrived at the corner store. *"You ok, Yolanda?"* he asks while trying to catch his breath. When I kept walking he grabbed my arm and made me face him. *"What does it matter to you? You probably think it's funny, anyway!* I shout at him while trying to free my arm from his grasp.

Tyrell tightens his grip and tells me to calm down. I didn't want to calm down. What I really wanted to do was to crawl under the Georgia red clay and bury myself. But since Tyrell was more powerful than me, I had to appear calm so that he would let go of me.

"It matters more than you know and I don't think it's funny either, Tyrell said after loosening his grip on my arm. What did he mean by that I thought? Not only did he answer my silent question but the next words out of his mouth took me by total surprise. *"It matters to me because I like you. The first day I saw you I thought you were cute. But Tyler told me you were his so I never said anything to you."*

The words I had just heard were shocking! Tyrell liked me and thought I was cute. Humph! Anybody can be cute but the fact that he liked me had my wheels turning. I never gave Tyrell a second thought because I was so into Tyler, plus they were brothers. I had to take time to process the new information but Tyrell had just given me a way to get back at Tyler.

"Tyrell, I'm flattered that you like me, but you are Tyler's brother; I don't know what I am supposed to say," I replied. As I stood there talking to Tyrell, I had to admit that he was quite attractive; although he was not as cute as Tyler. Tyrell stood about 5'11, with medium brown skin. He wore a low cut fade with thin sideburns. His teeth were pearl white and he had a slight dimple in his right cheek when he smiled. He had slanted dark brown eyes which seemed to close when he laughed. Any girl would be proud to be on his arm.

Tyrell responded by saying, *"Yolanda, I know who my brother is, but he's only been using you. He already has a girlfriend and plus he's too old for you anyway. All I'm asking for is a chance; can you give me a chance?"*

I knew what I was about to do was wrong, but I couldn't just let Tyler do me the way he did and get away with it. I told Tyrell I'd give him a chance, but I didn't tell him that I was only doing it to get back at Tyler. We started hanging out and I would deliberately show up at his house when I knew that Tyler was at home. I was hoping to make him jealous, but it didn't appear to be working.

One day I happened to show up at their house when Tyrell was not at home. Tyler came to the door and he was so rude to me that I cried all the way back home. He told me that I was stupid, immature and easy because I was messing around with his brother. He even went as far as to say that Tyrell was just with me because he had told him about me. *"Tyrell doesn't want your funky behind either. He's only with you because he can get some sex from you, and you too stupid to realize it!"* he yelled at me.

I was speechless all I could say was, *"I'm not easy and I don't want neither of you either!* I screamed back and left. The fact of the matter was I did want one of them. I wanted Tyler but it was obvious that he didn't want me, he probably never did. Then he tells me that Tyrell was only using me too! I didn't think I was easy, I knew what I was doing, I was trying to make Tyler jealous and my plan backfired! Tyler was right about one thing, I was stupid.

At fourteen years old daddy was still forcing himself on me. No matter how I tried to fight him off of me he yet managed to overpower me. My bedroom door did not have a lock on it, so I tried stuffing shoes under the bottom of the door to keep him from opening it. That didn't work. You can only have so many periods in a month, so I couldn't keep telling him I was on my period. Plus he was so greedy for sex that he would make me show him proof that my period was on. I wasn't sure what illness my mother had that made her not able to have sex with my daddy, but I sure wished she'd get better!

One night when I had just got out of the shower he met me in my room and pulled the towel out from around me. My mother was at the other end of the house so I tried to yell but before I could he placed his hand over my mouth and shoved me against the wall. He didn't do anything but look at me and whispered in my ear,*" I'll be back later."* He then released me and walked out. I just fell to the floor and cried. I was so tired of him messing with me, but what was I supposed to do?

Later that night of course he made good on his promise and returned to my room when my mother was sleep and forced his self on me. My mother snored loudly, so that is how he ensured that she was good and sleep while he was in my room. My room was on the opposite end of the house from theirs and you could hear her snoring in my room if my door was left open.

As long as he could hear her snoring he knew he was safe from being caught.

He had gotten to the point where he would fight me now when I tried to fight him back. If I would hit or pinch him, he would hit and pinch me back. When he got tired of me fighting him he would just apply more force by pinning my arm to the bed. Sometimes, I wouldn't even fight back, being that I wouldn't win anyway. I just lay there and prayed he would hurry up.

I threatened to tell on him if he didn't stop, but he just said my mother wouldn't believe me since she knew that I was having sex. I happened to get bold one night and snuck Tyrell into my house. While we were in the act my dad came into my room for his sexual gratification. He and I both got an unexpected surprise. He caught Tyrell and me sexing it up. All hell broke loose that night.

He started hollering about how I could disrespect his house like that." *This is a holy house and you disrespect our home like this!"* he yelled. Tyrell jumped up and started grabbing his clothes. I just sat up in the bed and pulled the covers up over my body. I was scared and ashamed both at the same time; I couldn't move. My dad blocked the door so Tyrell couldn't leave. He turned on the light and looked at Tyrell and threatened to send him to jail. *"How old are you anyway? You look way older than*

fourteen. Do you know how old she is? I'll have you put in jail!" He glared at Tyrell
I silently prayed that Tyrell wouldn't be dumb and tell him how old he really was. If daddy knew that he was eighteen then he may have followed through with his threat. Tyrell must have read my mind because he didn't tell.

My mother bust into the room looking like she had just seen a ghost. *"Oh, my goodness,"* She screeched. *Yolanda, how could you do such a thing?"* She came forward and just started hitting me anywhere she could with her hands. In the midst of the beating I hear Tyrell begging," *I'm sorry Mr. Shelton, please don't call the police, I promise I won't do anything like this again, just please don't call the police. Please!"* My dad told him to get out of his house and to never let him see his face around there again.

I didn't think my mother was ever going to stop beating me. I tried to block the blows but to no avail. She was a mad woman." *I can't believe you would do something like this, we didn't raise you this way, but you continue to bring disgrace to our home."* she yelled while looking for another place to hit me. I wondered if she would be this mad if I told her the only reason I got caught was because dad was coming back here to sex me up.

After she finished beating me they both told me that I was grounded and I could not talk on the phone or visit any of my friends after school. It wasn't like I had that many to start with. I felt like I was in continuous confinement anyway. So I didn't care. The only people I was allowed to visit were Honey and her cousin who lived across the street. I had to sneak and talk on the phone if I wanted to talk to anyone other than them anyway, so being grounded meant nothing to me.

The thing that stayed on my mind the most was that they kept saying this was a holy house, a place that God lived in. I had to wonder if God really lived there. Didn't he see what my dad was doing? Then again maybe I was sent there to take care of my dad's sexual needs, because nothing ever happened to him. Everybody thought we had the perfect family, if only they knew the real truth.

Tyrell made good on his promise. I never heard from him again. In spite of what Tyler had previously told me about Tyrell using me for sex, I really think he liked me. I don't believe it was all about the sex with him because sometimes we'd be together and he would just hold me and talk to me about his future. Tyler left in February of 1983 to join the army and Tyrell said he was thinking of going too.

I really missed seeing Tyrell, I missed Tyler too because I was in love with that man, but after what he did and said to me things weren't the same. As I think about it now I'm not sure if it was the sex or actually Tyler that I really missed. To me he was a good lover, better than Tyrell. Tyrell must not have been that experienced because he would get all nervous and would often be aiming for the wrong location or be trying to create a new one. I once told him while he was struggling trying to find the right place to enter," *Look, as far as I know I only have two places that you can go in, and right now you missing both of them."*

"You have a smart mouth to be so young. Well you guide me to where I am supposed to be, smarty," He replied. I didn't like touching him down there but I went ahead and placed him against me so he could enter me. I think he just liked me to touch him down there because he always seemed to clumsily miss his place. However, Tyler always knew what to do. The other difference between the two was that Tyrell would always hold me afterwards, but Tyler would just either go to sleep or rush me out the door.

After the incident with Tyrell I was the talk of our community for a while, since it was so small everybody had heard about what had happened with Tyrell and me. I was embarrassed to go to school but no one said anything to my face about it. But I knew they talked about me behind my back because Honey told me some of the things her friends said. It bothered me for a moment but not for long because I wasn't the only person having sex. There was a sixteen-year-old girl at school that got pregnant and soon all gossip turned towards her and off of me. I felt bad for her but was glad the spotlight was no longer on me.

In the summer of 1983 we moved from Georgia to Troy, Alabama. It was just as small as Lafayette. I just knew I was going to hate this place. However, just like Georgia I ended up having good and bad experiences . We moved next door to a family that had two children named Princeton and LaShaun their dad was a Baptist preacher. How ironic that two preachers would move next door to each other.

I met Princeton one day while he was helping my father do some things around the house. Princeton was a few months older than I was. He turned fifteen in August and my birthday was in November. It seemed that Princeton and I immediately had this attraction or connection to each other but I guess both of us were too scared to say anything. So we would always just tease each other. I liked Princeton's family they were very nice people and seemed not to be so strict on their children, not even LaShaun, Princeton's sister. LaShaun and I became fast friends also; she was easy to talk too and very funny. Even though they were PK kids they were allowed to participate in school activities and go to the school parties and everything. I often wished that their parents were my parents.

Even at fifteen I couldn't do anything but go to church. I envied the girls that could stay after school and play sports or be in the different clubs. I on the other hand had to get on the long yellow school bus and go home. I hated my life.

One day I deliberately missed the bus so I could stay for a talent show the school was having. It was the talk of the school and everybody was going. My other friend Keisha, asked me was I going to the talent show. I told her no because my parents would not allow it. Plus I knew they would fuss about having to come and get me after school. I knew that from the one time I accidentally missed the bus.

She told me the day before the talent show, *"I'll get you a way home if you stay. Just tell them you had to make up a test or something."* I agreed to attend the show, but I didn't know how I was going to pull it off. I waited until the buses left the school and then went to the office and called home.*" Mom, I had to stay after school to take a test that I failed, but Keisha said her mother would bring me home."* Before I could finish she started fussing about why I failed the test and why you have to take it after school and so on. *"Did you forget we have church tonight?"* she asked, sounding agitated.

I totally had forgotten about church, I had been too busy plotting a way to attend the talent show. I thought to myself that I go to church all the time, but I had never been to a talent show. *"No, mom I didn't forget about church, but I have to take this test over or I might fail the class."* I lied. I hated lying to her, even though I felt I had a good reason too. She told me that I better hurry and get myself home or else. What does *'or else'* mean? I thought. Or else she was coming to the school to pick me up? I doubt it. Or else she would beat the Jherri curl juice out of my hair if I didn't hurry and get home? Yeah! That would be the case especially if she had to stay home and miss church. They weren't about to leave me at home alone, as if I were a baby.

As I hung up the phone, I asked God to forgive me for lying. I still believed all liars would go to hell. My daddy preached fire and brimstone all the time; I felt he was talking to me, since he would always look at me when he said it from the pulpit.

The talent show was very good, I enjoyed it so much. I was glad that I went. However, it lasted two hours and I know that my mom wouldn't believe that the test took two hours. Keisha had arranged for one of her older brother's friends, Kenny to take me home. Both Kenny and Keisha's brother had come to the talent show. She said he lived near my house and would take me home.

I didn't know Kenny and was a little scared about riding with him, but she said it was ok. Keisha's brother was about twenty-years old so Kenny must have been around the same age. He was tall and light brown complexion with a mustache. He looked kind of scary to me, but since Keisha knew him I went ahead and got in the car plus I didn't have any other way home.

Kenny asked me exactly where I lived and I told him and he drove off from the school parking lot. He headed towards my house but said he had to pee real bad and pulled off down this dirt road. I lived in the rural part of Troy so we were already on a country road and the houses seemed miles apart. I didn't think anything about it when he said he had to pee. I just thought he was going to run in the bushes, pee and come back out. That was not the case.

He pulled off down the dirt road and turned the car off and looked at me. He was making me nervous." *Why you looking at me. I thought you had to use the bathroom?"* I asked nervously. He slid closer to me in the car as I moved as close to the passenger door of his Monte Carlo as possible. He placed his hand against my cheek and asked, *"Do you have some gas money?"*

Keisha didn't say anything about me having to have some gas money. All I had was two dollars of the hush money my daddy had given me, and I had to use that to pay for lunch. I told him I only had two dollars. *"That's not enough to fill my tank up, you need more than that."* he said while inching closer to me. My heart was pounding as I pondered how I was going to get home. I didn't have anything else to give him.

"I don't have anything else to give, but the two dollars should be enough to get me home." I said while never taking my eyes off of him. He told me I was being selfish because I was only worried about me getting home and not about how he was going to get home too. I sure wish Keisha had told me about needing gas money. I wouldn't

have eaten lunch if I had known I needed to pay him gas money.

Kenny grabbed the back of my head and said, *"Stop playing around with me, you know what I want. Either you give it to me or you can walk home!* He roared at me. It was mid January and the weather had already turned cold and it was dusk dark outside. I knew I couldn't walk the five miles or so to my house. I just sat there and started crying as he pulled up the brown wool skirt I had on. I tried to push his hands away but he grabbed my hand and looked at me and then looked out the front window. The look he gave let me know either I let him do what he wanted to do or either I would be left out in the cold, alone on this dirt road.

I didn't have enough will power to get out the car. As he roughly pulled my panties off, I pleaded with him not to do this! He was not hearing me. He climbed on top of me and reached over and reclined my seat. While he was trying to unzip his pants, I tried to push him off of me, but he didn't bulge. He yanked me by my hair and told me I was making it harder on myself if I kept trying to fight him. It reminded me of the times when I would try and fight my daddy off me, it was a no win situation.

With a strong force he rammed his penis into me; he just kept doing it over and over and over again. It hurt so badly, I didn't think he was going to ever stop. I lay pinned against the seat with my legs barely open as he forcefully raped me. I looked up into the cloth interior of his car and cried until he was finished. I was numb all over. I couldn't believe this was happening to me.

As if he hadn't just committed a crime, he slid back into the driver's seat, zipped up his pants and crank up the car and drove off. I picked up my panties and put them in my coat pocket. I didn't bother to put them back on. I pulled down my now wrinkled skirt and looked out the window. I wondered what had I done to deserve this? Surely, a lie didn't warrant such a hideous punishment.

We rode the rest of the way in silence. He stopped three houses down from mine to let me out. *"Thanks, I enjoyed it,"* he smiled. As if I had just served him his favorite meal. Did he not know that he just raped me? There was nothing enjoyable about that for me. Yet, I couldn't say anything because if I had not lied I wouldn't have been in this situation; I was partly to blame. He waited for me to get out and drove off.

I slowly walked the short distance to my house. I knew momma would be mad about me taking this long to get home. However, when I explained what happened then she would know it wasn't my fault. Well maybe it is my fault, I thought as I walked to our front door. If I hadn't been scheming in the first place then this wouldn't have happened to me; all because I wanted to go to a stupid talent show. What my daddy said is true, *"vengeance is mine, sayeth the Lord, and I will repay."* He used to say it doesn't pay to do evil because the Lord will get you back. I guess being raped is the retribution for lying to my mother.

The lights were on in the house but our car was gone so I knew momma was in the house and daddy was gone to church. I was right because as soon as I opened the door she met me at the door with an extension cord and went to beating me.

My purse and book fell to the floor as I tried to block her swings. I fell to the floor from the pain of the cord hitting me all on my back and from pure distress. I couldn't believe after what had just happened to me that I was being beat; not even able to plead my case first.

I hovered on the floor with my hands over my head as she continued to beat me with that brown extension cord. Something within me broke, I wanted to die! *"I just can't take this anymore!"* I cried within myself. I screamed out in agony both from the pain of the beating and from the turmoil I felt in my heart.

I don't know when she stopped beating me, somewhere between the beginning and the end I withdrew myself mentally from the hurt I was feeling. *"Yolanda, do you hear me?"* she shouted at me. I looked up with tear stained eyes as she was again yelling for me to get up. It appears she had been looking out the front window when she saw me get out the car. She was able to get a glimpse of Kenny as he drove by. From her point of view it appeared that I had been sneaking around with him. Not to mention that my hair was frazzled, my skirt was wrinkled and twisted and it was 7:30 p.m.

I may have thought the same thing too, but I at least would have given my child a chance to give me an explanation. She just assumed I was sneaking around with Kenny and that couldn't have been farther from the truth. No doubt I lied to her, but did I deserve to be raped? Then turn around and come home to one of the worse beatings of my life. I don't think so.

I didn't even bother to tell her what Kenny had done to me. She had already determined that I lied to her about having to take a test. I didn't deny it. When she accused me of having sex with Kenny, I wanted to tell her what really happened but decided against it. I had already been beat for my alleged sin so I saw no need in trying to prove myself innocent. Plus she didn't believe me when I tried to tell her about daddy, she certainly wasn't going to believe me now; especially after she knew I had lied to her already.

She told my daddy about it once he got home and I got to hear all over again how I've been troubled all my life. To make matters worse, dad decides to come by my room that same night for his usual custom. *"Since you like opening your legs, you might as well open them again,"* he said as he forced himself upon me. I didn't have the strength to fight him off, I didn't even try. It was times like these that I wished I knew my *'real parents'*. Who and where are the people that birthed me into this world? I wish I knew. I just wanted somebody to come rescue me but it never happened.

I think my dad began to get scared that I might actually tell on him, so he started promising me money if I did not tell. As a teenager I was always asking for money for school supplies, clothes and to buy junk food. I didn't get an allowance, so when he promised me money I was gratified. Although I knew it was wrong to take it, I felt I might as well get something for my troubles. He was going to forcefully get what he wanted anyway so why shouldn't

I. Plus he wasn't paying me for the sex, he was paying to keep me quiet about the sex.

I quickly realized that the measly $5.00-10.00 that he gave me didn't compensate for the misery that I felt afterwards. The money didn't change how I felt; I still hated when he came into my room. I hated him. I once told him that he could keep the money; I just wanted him to leave me alone. He told me, *"Take it anyway because once a whore always a whore. It didn't matter if she was paid or not."* Then he threw $10.00 on my bed and walked out.

So now he thinks I'm a whore. It is funny that in the presence of others he would brag about how smart I was and how I was going to be something in life. However, sometimes when we were alone he'd call me names and make me feel so low about myself. I was confused; he had me thinking that my only purpose in life was for sex. Of course he would remind me from time to time that I was sent there for that reason. I guess that is why I so easily gave into Tyler and Tyrell. Sex was all I knew.

My daddy never stopped preaching nor did he ever stop nudging me to get saved and turn my life over to God. He'd quote, *"Seek the Lord while he may be found. One day you will seek the Lord and he won't answer you."* I began to think that God was already hiding from me, because he hadn't rescued me from my daddy's vile ways.

Church still remained a haven for me. I enjoyed going and being a part of the love that I felt while I was there. Again, music was a part of me and when I sang, I felt like a weight was being lifted from my shoulders. Sometimes, I would be singing and the tears would just flow. The audience would think I felt the spirit or was catching the Holy Ghost. It wasn't that, not all the time anyway. Sometimes I was just over whelmed with emotion but there were times when I did feel the presence of God.

Even if the Holy Ghost was about to fall on me, I believe it would change its mind once he saw Sis. Sims standing there. I'm sure the Holy Ghost smelled that breathe! She was the head usher and would always be the one to come fan you or bring tissue when you started shouting . She loved her job, she'd fan me and with that sour smelling breathe say, *"Let the Lord use you, baby. Just let him have his way."*

I would know clearly when I wasn't in the spirit because I would quickly want to reply, *"Why don't you USE Listerine and let it have its Way with your Breathe."* Of course I never said that but it is what I was thinking. And I knew

Sis. Sims meant no harm, even though she was causing much harm to my nose!

Many funny things would happen at church and laughing always made me feel better too. One time we had a visitor come to church. I guess she hadn't been to church much in her lifetime. When Daddy said, *"Go to the book of Lamentations."* The visitor quickly stood up and said with all sincerity, *"Where do I get that book at, I only have this here 'Holy book'* and she waived an old motel bible in the air as proof. The whole church went silent, even daddy looked as if he were about to lose his composure. It was too funny! One of the members went over and helped her find the scripture. Daddy was able to go on with his message, but I saw several people with their head hung down laughing; including me.

My most memorable incident happened one Sunday when one of our members went to the altar for prayer. She raised her hands as most people do when they are being prayed for. When she raised her hands her white, cotton half slip fell down onto the floor. No one moved everybody just sat there and looked. It wasn't like you could stop the preacher in the midst of his prayer so she could pick her slip up. I'm not sure if she realized it had fell but she kept her hands up until the preacher was finished praying for her. When she turned to go to her seat, Sis. Sims our lead usher, pointed down to the floor for her to pick up her slip.

I was embarrassed for her. She just bent down picked up her slip and went back to her seat. Those are just a couple of the funniest things that I've seen during my lifetime of church. If it wasn't for church I don't think that I could have survived as long as I did. Living at home seemed unbearable at times. Even still church was just a temporary release for me; it didn't erase the troubles I had to deal with on a regular basis but it helped take the edge off.

My parents thought I was too young to date and they barely let me talk on the phone to any boys. Even though they knew I wasn't a virgin anymore they still would not condone me having a boyfriend. I think it was a double standard because when Donnie joined our church and took an interest in me they thought it was ok.

Here I am fifteen years old and Donnie was twenty-one years old. He had his own car and shared an apartment with his cousin. He claimed to be so saved and sanctified. I guess that is why my parents agreed to let me go out with him. I really wasn't that into Donnie but I was elated that I could date. Dating Donnie gave me something to do besides sit at home.

Momma started telling me how to act and how to dress like a lady and what men expected from young ladies and so forth. I thought it was a little too late for this conversation. I did act like a lady and I had no choice but to dress like a lady because they bought my clothes. I dressed like a lady, alright; an old lady.

All momma knew to buy was long skirts and turtle-neck sweaters. I barely got to wear pants. I used to wear those thick leg warmers with my skirts in the winter to keep my legs warm. The kids at school didn't have to pick on me because I picked on myself. I knew I looked like a 'black' Laura Ingles from 'Little House on the Prairie." The only difference was she was white with long wavy hair; and I was black with long Jherri curl hair.

What was considered my first real date was to Taco Bell one Wednesday evening before church. Donnie drove up in his old orange colored Datsun and came knocking at the door. I let my daddy open the door. I had heard a girl say one time, *"Never open the door yourself, and always make them wait a few moments."* If you make them wait then you won't seem desperate. So I made Donnie wait a few moments while I pretended to be finishing getting dressed.

Truth of the matter I had been dressed an hour before. Shoot! I didn't have anything to do but take a shower, change school clothes, and smear some Vaseline on my lips because I didn't wear make-up. I was dressed in a matter of fifteen minutes.

Daddy, Momma and Donnie were in the kitchen talking when I made my entrance. Donnie smiled like he had just found gold. Momma and Daddy both said I looked nice. It wasn't like they had never seen these clothes before, I've been wearing them for the last year. It seemed I only got to go shopping three times a year: the beginning of the school year, Christmas and Easter. I was lucky if I got any new clothes at the beginning of the school year. Momma would say, *"Ain't no need in buying all those new clothes, when I have to turn right back around and buy clothes for Christmas!"* She used to make me so mad when she said that!

The drive to Taco Bell was a short drive and in that time our conversation was very basic. *Where did you grow up? What you like to do? And of course church.* Donnie and I ate pretty much in silence. He seemed to be kinda shy. And since I really wasn't that much into him, I didn't have much to say either.
We talked more about our families and about school. He tried to change the subject by asking, *"How is your taco?"*

as he chewed his food. “Crunchy”, I replied. How the heck did he think it was? How do you ask somebody how there taco is. It wasn’t like it was a steak and he needed to know if it was cooked right. I already knew that he was not going to be a keeper, with him asking me stupid questions like that.

We finished eating and went to church. We ended up dating on a regular basis. Dating Donnie gave me something to do outside of being home and going to church. My parents thought that he might be my savior and deliver me from my wild side. What they didn’t know was that Donnie was the devil in sheep’s clothing. After our first couple of dates he had his hands all over me.

Many times after church we would go out to eat or go over to his house. His cousin and his girlfriend were always there and we knew they were sexing it. I guess Donnie didn’t want to feel left out. We started out just kissing, he was a great kisser and his kisses alone excited me. After the kissing we just ended up going all the way.

“Oh, Yolanda, ooh Yolanda” he would always say in my ear. In my head I was wishing that he shut up because he sounded like a little punk. He ended up being an ok, lover because I experienced my first ‘Big O’ with him. The sad part about it was he wasn’t even trying too, it just happened. And at first I didn’t know what had happened.

We were on the couch having sex and he was doing his usual chant of my name and in a slapdash fashion gyrating around. I was really lying there bored but letting him do his thing since he seemed to get so much pleasure out of it. All of a sudden my *'ms kitty'* gets this wonderful sensation. As he continued to push up against me the sensation increased and then it felt as if it burst. The explosion was the best part.

Silly me, I didn't even know what an orgasm was. I had heard about it before but never gave much thought about it. Donnie just kept doing what he was doing; he was trying to get his own explosion. He didn't even know I had just had an orgasm. While he was reaching his explosion I laid there wondering what had just happened and hoping that he could make it happen again.
He didn't, well not that night he didn't.

On the way home is when I finally realized that I'd had an orgasm. I kept pondering in my mind until the light bulb went off. *"Duh! You just experienced the 'Big Boom' that every woman wants to experience and you didn't even know what it was."* I said to myself. After that it was me that wanted to have sex all the time. Donnie was happy to oblige. He thought he was "the stuff"! It wasn't the sex I wanted but I was chasing after that amazing explosion!

To my dismay, it never happened again, not with Donnie anyway.

Donnie and I dated for about six months and he had asked my parents if he could marry me. I was fifteen in the tenth grade and he wanted to get married. To my disbelief my parents said yeah, but he had to wait until I was finished with school. That meant two years before we could get married. He bought me an engagement ring and everything. In my heart I knew it wouldn't happen because I was not in love with Donnie. He was a nice guy but I wasn't into him like he was into me. I couldn't believe that my daddy was willing to let me get married anyway. The only good thing I could see from it was getting out of daddy's house; other than that, I didn't want to marry Donnie.

Marriage meant that I would no longer be under his control and he couldn't sex me up any more. Donnie said that he loved me and I told him that I loved him too, but I didn't. I didn't know what else to say, it didn't seem nice to say, *"but I don't love you"* so I said what he wanted to hear.

During the time that we were dating I had met this guy named Michael who I thought was the finest thing I had ever laid eyes on. He was light-skinned with hazel green eyes. He stood about 5'11, slim build with a very defined body. I met him at a field and track meet we had at school. It happened to be during school hours or else I wouldn't have been able to go.

Michael lived in a nearby city called Brundidge, Alabama. He actually was out of school but had come to see his sister run track. My neighbor LaShaun introduced us, she knew Michael from her friends in Brundidge.

We hit it off right away. I couldn't stop looking in his eyes. I had never seen anyone with green eyes before. He asked me for my phone number but I told him my parents were strict and I couldn't accept phone calls from boys.

"Can I write you then?" he asked in his southern accent. I didn't think that was safe, either because the mailman delivered mail before I got home from school. Therefore, I told him to mail it to my girlfriend, Keisha's house. We exchanged addresses and began communicating through mail. Keisha would bring the letters to school and I would write him back and mail them to him.
I fell in love with him just from reading his letters.

Michael was a *'round the way guy'*. I could tell he had experienced many things during his eighteen years of life. He would be considered a 'rough neck,' I guess that was why I was so intrigued with him. Donnie happened to find one of his letters in my purse when he was looking for a pen one day. He read the letter and confronted me about it. I didn't even try to lie about it; I was tired of him anyway.

"How could you do this to me? We are supposed to get married," he said in a pitiful voice. He actually was hurt over the situation. I was hurt too, hurt that he found out. I didn't know how I would have broken up with him, but I knew I wouldn't have married him. I wasn't ready for marriage at least not to him and plus I didn't love him.

I told him I was sorry and that I didn't mean to hurt him. I really didn't. He asked for his cheap ring back and left. He left it up to me to break the news to my parents. Oh, brother! I knew that would be harder than him finding out about Michael and me. I didn't tell them right away. My daddy asked me why Donnie hadn't been around in awhile and knew I might as well tell them the truth.

They hit the ceiling when I told them the truth about how he found a letter from Michael. Of course they wanted to know who Michael was; how did I meet him and so on? It didn't matter about all of that because I knew they weren't going to let me see him anyway.

Momma told me I'd made the mistake of my life.*" you don't realize what you have done. That boy loved you. He was a good man; he had a job and would have done anything for you. But you throw it away over somebody you barely know!"*

Daddy had to throw his two cents in by saying, *"Donnie is saved. Is this boy you talking about saved? He sounds like he just out to have sex like most of these young kids are. I don't know when you will ever learn some sense."*

I wanted to scream, *'he was sexing me up just as much as you are daddy!'* But I held it in. Instead I looked at both of them and asked with a harsh voice, *"How do you know, unless you give him a chance? Doesn't the bible say don't judge?"* I couldn't remember what else went along with that *'don't judge part'* but I knew the bible said something about judging. Daddy was always throwing the bible at me so I figured I'd throw it back at him.

I guess what I said hit a weak spot because they agreed to let Michael come to the house and visit. Whew! I was astounded that they actually agreed to let him visit. One step at a time, I couldn't ask for too much too soon.

I still didn't have Michael's phone number we were just writing to each other. One time he did drive up to Troy to see me. It was only about a thirty-minute drive. He came to the school and ate lunch with me. I don't know what he seen in me because I know he could have had any girl he wanted but here he was having lunch with me, 'black Laura Ingles'.

A week had passed before Michael came to visit. Momma and Daddy had to approve of the day he came and how long he could stay and everything. They made it seem as if they were the wardens and I was the jail inmate. Sadly to say it was the truth. I was an inmate in my own home. Inmates did get an hour of recreation time a day. That is more than what I could say about me. I wonder if church is considered a recreation in jail, because if not, jail might not have been such a bad place.

Michael and I set the date for a Friday evening around five o' clock. He had to be gone by eight o'clock; even though it was a weekend night. They acted as if I had school the next day. However, I was still elated that he was going to get to visit, so I didn't gripe about the time. I actually thought it was a decent time frame, considering the strictness of my parents.

Donnie had called one time to see if we could get back together but I said "*No* but I still want to be your friend." He hung the phone up on me so I figured he didn't want to be friends. It was hard seeing him at church but I quickly got over that because Michael had the center of my attention. Donnie started dating some other girl about two months later. I think he was trying to make me jealous. I wasn't. She came up pregnant and everybody in the church realized that he wasn't so saved after all. Momma and daddy never talked about it. I'm sure they wondered if Donnie and I had sex too; but I won't be the one to tell.

The Friday that Michael was to visit, I stayed busy by cleaning the house. I was so jubilant that my heart felt like it was turning flips. Momma and Daddy acted like it was no big deal. After I finished cleaning, I searched through my meager selection of clothing to select what to wear. Just looking through my closet caused my emotional high to subside. Nothing in my closet seemed to be appropriate. I wanted to look sexy but conservative. Conservative was not a problem; it was the sexy look that I had to create.

Since I didn't wear jeans, I decided on a slim fitting black knit skirt with the quarter length sleeve tunic to match. Black is always an attractive color to wear so I figured I couldn't go wrong. My hair was the easiest thing to put together. I wore a wavy-looking Jherri curl so it wasn't much to do to it. I decided however to part it on the right side and pull it back behind my ear and let the rest of it hang. I had shoulder length hair so I usually wore a part any way to keep it out of my face.

Michael called around three o'clock to let me know that he was still coming. The fact that he thought enough to call and confirm our date was a sweet and thoughtful gesture. I liked that about him.

Through dinner daddy kept quizzing me about Michael's parents. I told him what little I did know. Michael had told me that his father, Nathan had passed away, and he lived with his mother, Daisy. He also had one brother and two sisters that lived with them. That is all I knew. *"What did you say his last name is?"* daddy asked, chewing on a piece of fried chicken breast. "His last name is Houston, and they live in Brundidge. I answered annoyingly. Daddy swore that he knew some Houstons and thought they were related. *"Yeah, I know David, Cheryl, and green-eyed Larry Houston. They're grand-mother is my daddy's third cousin." he exclaimed.*

As I ate and continued listening to daddy I became petrified that Michael and I could be related; especially when he mentioned green-eyed Larry. I didn't know green-eyed Larry, but I knew green-eyed Michael; my Michael had hazel green eyes. This could not be happening to me; we could not be cousins. I couldn't wait to nullify the possibility of us being related once Michael arrived.

At exactly 4: 51 P.M; a newly waxed grey Delta 88 Oldsmobile pulled into our driveway. My stomach and heart were doing somersaults. Mom and daddy were seated in our modest living room, which I had previously cleaned and neatly rearranged. With anticipation I opened the front door and stood in the doorway until he reached our porch. I swiftly unlocked the screen door and let him in!

He walked in with a glimmer in his eyes and smiled as he leaned forward a bit. I think he was going to welcome me with a kiss until he noticed my parents sitting there. He quickly turned his head in their direction and said hello. *'Why did they have to be sitting there?'* I murmured to myself. After the formal introductions, Michael and I went into the adjoining kitchen. I guess that is why momma and daddy went into the living room because they would have a good view of what we were doing.

I offered Michael some red Kool-aid. You know us black folks didn't drink anything but red Kool-aid or tea; and tea is what we drank on Sundays. He declined the kool-aid, but I fixed some for myself. I had to have something to do with my hands.

Michael looked very nice in his Levi blue jeans and Yellow Izod pullover shirt that clung to his toned frame. He was not very muscular but I could tell that he worked out a bit. Michael stood about 5'11, that's not as tall as I usually like but he was taller than me and that's all that mattered. I was about 5'5 tall and to me that was short. Therefore, I was attracted to tall men. I couldn't imagine having to bend down to get a kiss. No! I couldn't have that, and in Michael's case I didn't have too.

Our conversation was kind of reserved in the beginning and then it progressed until he had me doubled over in pain from laughter. He told me how his brother had to go to the emergency room because his lips were glued to a Coke can. Michael said that often times they would leave an opened can of coke in the refrigerator only to later find that someone would have drank the remaining contents. Of course the guilty culprit would not confess.

Michael decided to line the top of the can with crazy glue so that whoever was drinking the Coke would be caught. It just so happened that one day less than five minutes after he put the glue laced coke can in the refrigerator that his brother came outside with the can glued to his lips. Michael said he hadn't thought about what would happen if someone's lips were stuck. He just wanted to know who was drinking up his Coke. Fortunately, the doctor was able to free his lips with no permanent damage. His brother was mad at first but he said they were laughing about it by the end of the day. Now that was funny, too bad I didn't have any funny sibling stories to tell. I had stories to tell but they weren't the ones he would want to hear; nor did I want to tell them.

As it was nearing 8:00 I started feeling sad and wishing that I could turn back the hands of the clock. I wasn't ready for him to leave; I needed more time with him. Michael made me feel alive and I haven't felt that way in a long time. I secretly crossed my fingers under the table while I asked him did he have any relatives named Cheryl or Larry Houston. *"Yeah, Larry Houston was my granddaddy. How do you know him?"* he quickly replied.

I felt faint and felt like I would have fainted if it hadn't been for my chair holding me up. This can't be happening to me, we just can't be cousins. *No! No!* I silently screamed to myself. I looked him straight in the eyes and said, *"You are not going to believe this, but we are cousins. Your granddaddy and my daddy are cousins. So that makes us cousins too!* I saw the blood as it rushed from his face; all of a sudden he looked pale.

Though we were distant cousins', cousins were family and you can't date your family.

While we both were sitting there speechless over the revelation of this devastating news, a smile suddenly appeared on my face. *"Why are you smiling, Yolanda? He asked." This isn't funny at all.* I couldn't stop smiling as I told him that it didn't matter that my daddy and he were blood related, because I was adopted. Therefore, I wasn't really related to him. As soon as I told him, he started grinning too. *"Good, that means you can be my girlfriend."* He said while reaching for my hand. *"Yep, I can be your girlfriend"* I exclaimed as I placed my hand in his.

"Yolanda! Do you see what time it is?" My mother asked from the living room. Mercy me! I thought as Michael and I stood up, she wouldn't even let me have an extra minute. The clock on our stove read exactly 8:00. I walked Michael to the door and he told my momma and daddy goodnight, and promised to call me later. Today was one of the best days of my life.

Before, I could get the door closed good, my daddy stated," *I told you that boy related to them Houston's. I knew it when he walked in here with those green eyes like green-eyed Larry. I bet Larry is his granddaddy.* Had he been ease dropping on our conversation or what? He couldn't wait to rub it in. He went on to say that it was a good thing that we were related because those Houston's were not good people.

Before I knew it I replied, *"It must run in the blood."* Meaning that since they were related he wasn't a good person either. *"Don't be getting smart,"* my mother yelled at me. I wasn't being smart I was just stating the facts and she would know that if she would just wake up and look around. The evidence was right under her nose but she couldn't or wouldn't see it. *"What did Michael have to say about you being kin?"* my daddy asked with a smirk on his face. And with a smirk on my face, I replied, *"There was nothing for him to say. We are not related. I'm adopted remember?"* and I walked past him and went into my room. I don't know what had gotten into me, but I was getting bolder by the minute. It was as if I didn't care what happened next. Normally, I wouldn't have said anything or used more subtleness with my choice of words, but recently I said what was on my mind.

They complained about me seeing Michael but I put up such an argument that they relented. I told them I felt it was double standard to allow me to date a grown man, seven years older than me because they liked him; but not allow me to date a person closer to my age because they didn't like him. Either I could date or I couldn't;

which one was it? Realistically, it was too late to say I couldn't date since they had allowed me to see Donnie, so they had to give in.

They were hurt over the fact that I said I wasn't related to them or to Michael. I understood their pain, but the truth of the matter was that I wasn't related to them. There was no blood relationship between us at all. Honestly, I didn't even feel connected to them. I guess emotionally I had separated myself from them because of what was going on with my father. I was in my own world. I had created a temporary place of solace in my mind. This was necessary if I were to remain sane. Many days I felt I was going to crack up, but somewhere I found strength to go on.

Although, my parents allowed me to continue to see Michael they still had their restrictions. He mostly had to come to our house to visit and if we went anywhere he had to have me home before it got dark. I was so fed up with all their rules that I didn't know what to do. I just wanted to be out of that house but there was nowhere for me to go or so I thought.

Dad was still coming in my room ever so often at night and having his way with me. I still would try to fight him off of me but of course I would lose because he was so much stronger. Many times I thought about blurting the truth to my mom but I didn't for fear of hurting her. I don't know what hold Dad had on my mother but I knew she couldn't survive without him. She depended solely on him. She never worked and because she was a sickly woman I know she needed him. The sad part about it was that even though he was doing all these things to me, a part of me still loved him. If the truth be told, I was dependent upon him too. If I didn't live with the Shelton's where else would I live? It was a hopeless situation.

One day Michael and I were talking and he asked me to go stay with him in Brundidge. I looked at him like he was crazy. *"What do you mean come stay with you? You know mom and dad would never allow that!"* I shouted to him. *"You're right, so don't tell them, just run away and come live with me!* He replied as he looked into my eyes. I could tell that he was serious by the way he looked at me but I still had to ask, if he were serious. *"Yes! I am serious!"* he replied back. *"You can live with me and my sister and her boyfriend."* Now I know it was a crazy idea, but at the time it sounded like the best thing in the world to do. So like a dummy I said, *"OK!"* We planned for me to run away on the last day of school. He would pick me up from school and take me to Brundidge.

My heart was running a mile a minute as I was packing my overnight bag. I stuffed everything in there that I could. I knew I couldn't sneak out the house with a suitcase; therefore I had to get it all in an overnight bag. The day I was leaving, I told my parents goodbye as I usually did and ran to the bus stop. Whew! I made it to the bus without any setbacks. School went by in a blur as I anticipated Michael coming to get me. When the bell rang, I swiftly ran to my locker got my bag and headed to the door. Michael was sitting outside waiting as he promised.

Michael got out the car and took my bag and put it in the backseat. I skipped to the passenger's side and got in the car; off into the sunset we went. I was nervous because I was wondering what mom and dad would think when I didn't get off that bus. Nonetheless, I was just happy to be with Michael.

His sister Andrea and her boyfriend Mitchell welcomed me with open arms. They had just moved into their own two-bedroom apartment and told Michael and I that we could have the extra bedroom. Both Andrea and her boyfriend were 25yrs old and they had a son that was six months old. Michael's family was very close, they did everything together, and their mother Daisy was cool. She did not question me about being there with Michael and she didn't say anything about Michael drinking a beer in front of her. I couldn't believe she was really their mother; my parents would have killed me and hand delivered me to hell if I even thought of drinking a beer!

Michael had a job at one of the fast-food restaurants so sometimes whenever he would have to go to work I would go with him and sit in one of the booths. He would bring me out free food and sit with me during his breaks. I was having so much fun being with my baby. He was so sweet to me. He was so into me that he wanted me everywhere he went. He was proud to have me as his girlfriend and I was just as proud to have him as my boyfriend.

I was enjoying myself so much that I forgot that I had run away, that is until the police showed up at Andrea's door a week and a half after I ran away and asked did she know a Yolanda Shelton. Michael and I were in the bedroom sleeping when she knocked on the door to tell us the police was looking for me. I nearly panicked to death; I thought I was going to jail! The police said my parents had been looking for me and had informed them that I may be with a young man by the name of Michael Houston. Voila! And there I was, standing there wondering what would happen next. The officer told me that unless I resisted they would not have to use cuffs but I had to go with them until my parents came to get me.

Salty tears streamed down my face and connected under my chin as I kissed Michael goodbye. He told me he loved me as he watched the officer place me in the back of the police car. I had never been in a police car before and felt like a criminal as the door was closed. As we rode to the juvenile detention facility I knew I was in big trouble. I knew I was going to be beat horribly. I was positive that both mom and dad were full of rage because of what I had done. I could already hear the scriptures dad was going to quote to me during the ride home. Although, I knew I was in big trouble I felt it was worth it all because I had lived ten days of freedom and peace! I didn't have to fight dad off at night, I was free to do whatever I wanted to do. Not to mention the thrilling sex Michael and I had!! So whatever consequences I had to suffer would be ok because the memories of the week would get me through.

Upon arriving at the Juvenile facility I was placed in this tiny room with only a small wooden stool until my parents arrived. They must have been around the corner because 15 minutes later a female officer opened the door and told me to follow her. I followed her to the front desk and there stood daddy. Don't you know he had the nerve to grab me and hug me! He acted as if he really missed me; maybe he did miss me, he missed not having me there to fondle and mess over, I thought to myself as he hugged me. Or maybe he was putting on a show for the officers; either way I knew he was eventually going to go off.

"Your Ma was worried sick", he said as he released his grip. I hung my head to avoid looking him in the eyes. Even though I hated to be back in his presence I knew I was wrong for leaving like I did. After he signed the release form we walked outside to the car. He told me mom was waiting in the car. Once we reached the car mom spoke to me as if she was picking me up after being away on vacation. Well, technically I was on vacation. I just didn't tell them I was taking one. *"Hi, Yolanda how have you been doing? I missed you."* she spoke in a calm soft-spoken voice. I couldn't believe my ears! Who are these people and where are the real Sheltons? Because I knew my mom and dad would never be this calm after what I did.

"I'm fine, mom" I answered while looking at the back of their heads. They looked like my parents but I still couldn't believe that they were so calm. I once heard my daddy preach and say sometimes the worse storm occurs when things seem so peaceful. Maybe my storm was brewing and I didn't know it. My mom did most of the talking while we rode home. She told me they had been so worried when I didn't come home and although she was upset about what I did, she understood.

Understood! She really had no idea I thought, she was just scared that something horrible had happened to me. I know she loved me, but she didn't have a clue how I felt housed up in the house all the time! She didn't know I felt used and misused and defiled after daddy would come into my room at night. I felt as if no one cared about me it was all about what Yolanda could do for someone else! I sometimes felt like a slave. Yolanda do this, and Yolanda come do that, please help with this. Yolanda! Yolanda! Sometimes I wished I could change my name! I was never asked to do, I was always told to do! And of course, as a child you didn't dare talk back or you might find yourself toothless. Ethel Shelton may have been sickly sometimes, but she had a strong backhand! So I never thought about saying no. And the word no certainly was not a word my dad liked to hear. If I said no to him it was a fight. Even to this day I am afraid to say NO! I don't like having to deal with the repercussions of not giving a person what they want. I was trained and manipulated to say 'Yes', especially where sex was concerned. I learned it was easier to say yes and give in. Saying NO! Only got me raped!

After the runaway ordeal mom and dad became a little more lenient concerning my dating Michael. They allowed him to take me on dates but I had to be home by 10p.m.

Once school started back he could not come visit me on a school night; I could only see him on the weekends. Sometimes his job prohibited him from coming on the weekends; sometimes we'd go weeks without seeing each other. He would call as often as he could but calling from Brundidge to Troy was long distance so I didn't always hear from him every day. I dare not think of calling to Brundidge too many times because I would be totally banned from the phone if I ran the phone bill up.

Dealing with the strict rules my parents enforced and not being able to see Michael every day started to cause a strain on our relationship. I knew that I wasn't seeing anyone else but I wasn't so sure about Michael. He had the freedom to do whatever he wanted to do and see whomever he wanted to see. I had started hearing rumors that he had a child on the way by some girl that lived in Brundidge. When I asked him about it he denied it and said people should stay out of his business. Being the young and naïve fifteen year old girl that I was, I believed him.

On July 4th 1985, my life began to change for the better, or so I thought. Michael and I along with his sister Andrea and her boyfriend Mitchell went to Six Flags of GA. It was about a 5-hour drive from Alabama. I knew we would never make it back to Troy by 10p.m. therefore, we had

Michael's mother Daisy to call and ask my mom if I could go to Atlanta with them to Six Flags. She convinced my mother that she would look out for me and that she would be there to chaperone. (That was a Lie!) Daisy never intended to go with us but she convinced my mom otherwise. My mom believed her and surrendered to Daisy's efforts and let me go. Daisy even rode with Michael to pick me up. I told you Michael's mom was the coolest. She was totally opposite my parents; which was working in my favor!

We had a blast at Six Flags! Michael and I rode almost everything. That was the best day of my life! Michael and I walked hand in hand; in between rides he was winning stuffed animals for me. Anything I asked for he got it for me. While we were walking through the park he asked me did I love him. *"Of course I love you; I thought you already knew that."* I said while smiling at him. *"Good!"* He answered, because I wanted to know for sure before I gave you this." *"Give me what?"* I asked as I looked at his hands. Michael had on his pinkie finger a small but cute diamond ring. I was smiling from ear to ear! *"Oh my gosh!"* I exclaimed. *"Where did you get that?" "It doesn't matter where I got it, it only matters if it fits",* he said to me as he slid the ring on my middle left hand finger. The ring seemed to be a perfect fit.

Michael asked if I would marry him. Marriage never crossed my mind, I was just happy to have a boyfriend! I said yes because it felt like the right thing to say but in my head I was thinking, *'My parents are never going to let their fifteen year old daughter get married, at least not to Michael anyway.'* Michael had just turned nineteen years old and he did not need his mother's permission to do anything and even if he did, Daisy probably would have said yes.

Andrea and Mitchell were happy for us but was questioning if we were ready and what would my parents say? I said I was ready because I just wanted to be with Michael. The next morning as we were driving back to Alabama, I just kept thinking what Mom and Dad would say. Michael didn't offer to come and ask my dad like Donnie had. I'm not sure if he knew to do that or not. I told them myself and they hit the roof! *"Married*!" My dad yelled, *"You kids are too young to be getting married and you haven't even known him that long!"* My mom agreed with my dad and said I wasn't old enough to get married. I knew they were not going to agree to it. Every reason for me not to get married was brought up such as me finishing school; Michael being able to support me; the fact we had only known each other six-months and everything in between. I had an answer for everything.

I promised I would finish school. I was an honor roll student and had no intentions of quitting. Michael still had his job at the restaurant; we were going to live with Andrea and Mitchell until we could get a place of our own. And I felt we knew enough about each other to get married. I knew enough to want to be his girlfriend so I knew enough to want to spend the rest of my life with him. However, nothing I said convinced them to allow me to get married. They even brought up the detail that Michael and I were related. *"We are not related!" I yelled, you are not my real mother or father, you adopted me remember?"* My mom was hurt by the malice words I uttered, I saw tears fill up in her eyes. It was then for the first time in my life that I actually realized that she really loved me. She actually thought of me as her daughter and not just some orphan child. It tore me apart to see her hurt and crying by what I said, but I could not take the words back at that moment.

Fact of the matter was, we really weren't related. I sometimes wished I were their blood daughter. Maybe then I would have felt connected to somebody, maybe I would have felt as if I belonged, maybe I wouldn't have still been getting fondled and sexed by my dad at fifteen; Maybe I would have felt loved and not searching for love through sex. Dwelling on maybe's and what if's didn't change the situation. As hurtful as the truth was, it was still the truth.

After the final word of 'NO' to getting married, Michael and I conspired on how we could still get married. My mom had always told me to never bring a baby home and shame the house. I knew being pregnant would devastate my dad simply because of his connection to the church. So I told Michael that if I got pregnant they would have no choice but to let me get married.
Every chance we could get we were having sex. Michael was such a skilled lover and not to mention well endowed. Even too this day I use some of the techniques that he taught me. I had only had consensual sex with three people. I did not know much when it came to sex. Michael brought a variety of spice to the bedroom. Sometimes he was good and slow, other times he would be rough and hard and sometimes we would role-play. I never turned him down whenever he was in the mood because I know I was in for a pleasurable moment. It was with Michael that I learned that there were other sexual positions other than the missionary style. I don't know if Michael's skill was a natural part of him or if he was taught from somebody else. Of course he says it came natural; I really didn't care as long as he kept making my temperature rise.

All the sex we were having I thought I would get pregnant right away. It didn't happen. I thought maybe I couldn't have kids. Not that I really needed one, but at the time a child was the answer to our problems. Dad was still sneaking into my room not as much but often enough. One time was too many. He still had this hold on me. I would threaten to tell mom and he would threaten me right back. *"You tell her and you'll regret it."* he would say. Or he would say, *"your ma, don't deserve to be hurt by you more than she already has."* I knew I had hurt her on more than one occasion and I didn't want to cause her more pain. He had me convinced that mom would think it was my entire fault. Therefore, I said nothing.

Once he caught an STD from me (crabs). I caught it from Michael, he was the one that told me I probably had it. That explained why I kept itching and scratching in my pubic area. Michael told me that he had went to the doctor and found out he had 'pubic lice' aka crabs. He told me he caught it from an unclean toilet seat and that he may have given it to me. He sounded so sincere and apologetic. Again, being the dumb naïve girl that I was I believed him.

I didn't even think that dad might have gotten it from me. I just went to the Health Department to get rid of it. The nurse gave me a cream to use that cleared it up in a few days. Later in the week dad came and told me he had it too. I was embarrassed about it but I couldn't help feeling that he deserved it, that's what he got for bothering me, I laughed to myself.

Since getting pregnant wasn't working, we decided to see if we could get married in another city or state. We learned that if under the age of 18 years old you could not be married without your parents consent in any nearby State. I would not turn sixteen until November and I would still need parental consent. I finally told Michael to just give it up because my parents were not going to sign. I was trapped in this home of emotional stress and turmoil. Michael was my only hope and I felt he was slowly drifting away.

Just after I had given up all hope of getting married, the unthinkable happened. On one of the nights that I was trying to fight off my dad, he said something to me that was nauseating but a solution to my problems. I so wanted to be free of him that I would agree to almost anything. I just wanted him to leave me alone so when he offered the proposition I pondered it and gave my answer.

My dad, the Right, Reverend, Dr. Leroy Shelton told me that if I stop fighting him and let him have his way with me one last time, he would convince mom to sign the papers for me to get married. Yep! I kid you not the so-called man of God that everybody at the church looked up too, propositioned his own daughter! He went on to say, I owed him for all the years he had taken care of me. He made it sound like he had taken in an unwanted stray dog. *"Surely, you can show me some appreciation, it's not costing you anything."* He seriously said.

I weighed the pros and the cons, either I could say No and continue to have to deal with him for two more years or I could say yes, and get the hell out of his house! I figured I was the one winning because I would be free of him and I would be with the man that I loved. Since he was going to keep taking advantage of me anyway, I might as well say yes and get it over with. He had taken my innocence as a child, technically he had taken my virginity, he had taken my happiness as a child; he had taken everything from me including my dignity. If he was giving me a chance to get away from him, then I was not going to let it pass me by.

I felt like a common prostitute after I said yes, but I felt that was my only way out of a horrible situation. Even to this day I am so ashamed of myself for even considering his offer, I don't think I ever forgave myself for what I did. But at the time, it seemed my only way out of an horrible situation. As I lay there and felt his calloused hands roaming my body, I let the tears fall from my face onto the beige pillowcase I laid on. I prayed God would forgive me for what I considered then as the unforgivable sin. I tried to think of Michael as he rammed his fingers in between my legs. *"Open up"* he whispered in my ear. I didn't move, he then pried open my legs and continued to move his fingers in and out of me. After a few moments he repositioned himself over me. I thought he was trying to position himself to enter me but instead he pushes his penis against my mouth. I was totally caught off guard because he had never done anything like that before. I pursed my lips together and moved my head away. I told him to stop because I changed my mind. I tried to push him off me but he placed his hands around my throat and told me, *" You better open your mouth or you will have hell to pay. I won't sign the papers and you'll have to deal with me forever. Plus you made a promise. Now open up!"* I was devastated because I knew he meant what he said. I can't explain the agony of him forcing himself down my throat. For a moment I thought I was going to die because I was gagging and couldn't breathe. He finally stopped, then pinned my hands over my head and pushed himself inside me and continued to rape me. I screamed and he slapped me and held one hand over my mouth until he finally released himself. I don't know what was worse, the guilt I felt for agreeing to such a repulsive act or feeling him release himself inside of me. What took all of about fifteen minutes seemed like ten hours. I was glad that it was finally over and I wouldn't have to deal with him anymore. As he rose up off me, he looked at me and said, *"Michael is getting some good stuff,"* and then he walked out and closed the door.

I dragged myself to the shower, got in and just let the hot water fall on me. As the water fell onto the shower floor, the tears fell from my eyes. I couldn't stop crying! I wanted the water to wash away the shame I felt. I don't know how long I stayed in the shower, but the cold water brought me back from my thoughts. I got out the shower and after drying off, I returned to my room and lie across the bed and gazed at the moon that shined through my window. I remember thinking," *If I could fly, I'd fly to the moon, a place far away from here.*" I must have finally drifted off to sleep because I was awakened by my mom's voice; she was yelling that breakfast was ready.

At the breakfast table, I listened to mom and dad's usual banter. They talked about the upcoming revival, the bills and their daily activities. Soon the attention turned to me when my mom asked, *"Yolanda, do you still want to get married?"* She spoke the words so matter-of-factly. I looked at her to see if she was serious before I answered, *"Yes, mom, I still want to get married." " Well, your dad and I have talked about it and we've decided that since you are so determined to be with Michael, that it's best you get married," she replied,* while spooning eggs into her mouth. Before I could respond, dad interjected, *"Plus, at least you won't be living in sin, God honors marriage and not fornicators."* He always had a way of saying things that made me feel like I was the lowest of the lowest.

I ignored his comment and asked mom, *'if they were going to sign the parental slip?'* She said *yes*. She didn't sound as if she really wanted to do it. That let me know that between the time dad left my room last night and early this morning, Dad had convinced her to agree to sign. Of course I know the reason for that happening. All I could think to say was thanks. I really couldn't believe they had agreed to it. After dad left my room I wasn't sure if he was going to really keep his word or if that was something he said just to get me to quit fighting him. I'm really not sure why he decided to let me get married, he could of reneged on the deal but I am glad he didn't; that would have made me feel worse.

I couldn't wait to call and let Michael know that we were finally going to be together. He couldn't believe it either. We agreed to get married as soon as I turned sixteen. My birthday was on November 11; we set our wedding date for November 16, 1985. You would think that after agreeing to letting us get married that my parents would let up on us. But they still held to their strict guidelines about having me home on time, they even told Michael he need to start going to church. He came with me a couple of times but didn't seem to impressed with the service; except when he heard me do the solo part for a song the choir was singing.

"Baby, I didn't know you could sing, wow! You sounded great," he exclaimed! I was elated that he enjoyed my singing. Singing was still the one thing I enjoyed doing. Music soothed my spirit whenever I was feeling down and out. I could let out all my pain through singing. I guess if it weren't for singing that I would have lost my mind. Maybe music was God's way of escape for me.

The church learned of my engagement and many of the members would come up and say congratulations but in the same breath they would say something like, 'marriage is hard work, or you haven't even lived your life are you sure you ready for marriage?' I know they meant well but I was not the first person that was getting married at a young age. I had heard stories about how my grandparents got married. My grandmother was fifteen and my grandfather was twenty-one years old and they were still married. I also knew a classmate that was getting married at sixteen and her parents were happy for her. Why couldn't everyone be happy for me as well?

I thought since I was getting married that I would have a bridal party like my cousin had when she got married. All her friends and family came and brought her gifts; everyone seemed so happy that she was getting married. But that didn't happen for me. All I got was some quilts and blankets from my mother. I was appreciative but could a sista' get some glasses or a gown or something? I couldn't even use the quilts and blankets until the wintertime. Give me something I can use every day! That's what happens when you have old timey, church folk as parents! But anyway, I humbly took the quilts and blankets and put them in my closet until I were to move to Brundidge with Michael.

School started back in mid August. I was happy to be going back to school because it gave me something to do during the day and it would pass the time until November. I told all my friends that I was engaged and getting married. They couldn't believe it but seemed happy for me, they told me how cute my ring was and that was pretty much all they had to say. They were too busy catching up on the latest gossip, I guess my getting married wasn't juicy enough to spend much time talking about.

The one thing they did comment on was my new look. I had my hair freshly redone in a Jherri curl, so my curls were still tight and cute. But the main thing was I had a new wardrobe. Michael loved to shop for me and would always buy me an outfit plus since my dad was retired I had started to receive money from his retirement. My dad would disburse money to me every month. Since I didn't go anywhere, I saved my money to buy clothes. Mom didn't say much about me buying pants but I could tell she didn't like it too much. They would prefer I continued to wear dresses and skirts for the rest of my life. However, since I would soon be married it was not much she could say. I tried wearing a little make-up, but that was pushing it too far. Mom would say that I looked like a Jezebel.

Jezebel was this woman in the bible that represented evil. I really didn't know what she looked like but anytime the church didn't like what a person had on, they referred to them as a *'Jezebel'*

It's a wonder I still believe in God especially since I wondered how such a loving God could allow an innocent child to be placed in a home of emotional and sexual abuse. And then my dad would use scriptures to keep me under his spell. It's true that you have the biggest influence on a child when they are young. Whenever I was at the breaking point, I felt God give me strength to go on. Though, I didn't understand his ways, I felt his presence with me.

The date for Michael and I to get married was fastly approaching. There really wasn't much preparation since we weren't having a wedding. We were going to the Justice of Peace in Troy. We had already gone to the Health Department to get our blood work done, which was required before a marriage license was given. Mom went and signed the parental form and I had that safely tucked away. I was doubtful that she was going to sign the parental form up until the very moment her signature was on the dotted line.

I noticed that LaShaun, my friend that introduced Michael and I had become very distant. She wasn't spending much time with me and she didn't say much while we were at school. That really wasn't like her and I couldn't figure out what her problem was. My feelings were hurt because I felt she should be spending, as much time with me as possible since she knew that in a few weeks I would be moving to Brundidge.

During our lunch break at school I went over to the table where she was sitting and asked if I could speak with her. She said yes. I asked her, *"LaShaun, why are you acting funny? Is it because I am getting married? Tell me what's going on with you?"* She looked me eye to eye and said without hesitation. *"Michael is cheating on you and I don't think you should marry him and he has a baby on the way!"* It took me a moment to process what she said to me. *"How do you know that LaShaun? Are you listening to your gossiping friends again?"* I spewed back at her. I knew Michael was not cheating on me; he had no reason too. Plus I knew he wouldn't do something like that, we were about to be married. Why would he be with someone else when he was marrying me? It didn't make sense.

LaShaun told me that her brother Princeton had seen Michael recently with some girl at a football game over in Dothan, Alabama. Princeton played on the high school football team; so I didn't question about him being at the game but I did question if Michael were there because he told me that he was working the Friday of that game. I told LaShaun that Princeton must be mistaken because Michael was working that night. *"Well, Princeton was pretty sure it was him and he said the girl was pregnant" Lashaun stated. He came home that night and told me, and you know he knows what Michael look like, since we knew him before you did. Don't forget that I was the one that introduced you guys."* I didn't care what LaShaun or Princeton had to say I did not believe that Michael was seeing someone else or that he had somebody pregnant.

LaShaun, said she didn't know how to tell me so she just stayed out of it and kept her distance. I couldn't wait to get home to call Michael and tell him what LaShaun had told me. In the beginning I may have believed that Michael was seeing someone else because my parents had such stern restrictions on me, but now that we were getting married and I had a little more freedom I refused to believe what I was hearing was true. If he had someone else he would never have asked me to marry him. But who was the girl that Princeton had seen Michael with? Neither of his sisters was pregnant, so it wasn't Andrea or Jamie his other sister. I tried to recall all the family members and friends he had introduced me to and no one came to mind.

I called Michael as soon as I got home to ask him about what I heard. To my surprise he didn't deny that he went to the game. He said that he was scheduled to work that night but when he went in at five o clock his manager sent him home because they had too many people on the schedule. Since he had free time he drove to the game, his excuse for not calling me was because he knew my parents wouldn't let me go to the game on such short notice. (he was probably right) *"But who was the girl, Michael?"* I questioned. *"Oh! That was just Tina, one of my old class mates, we ran into each other after I got to the game."* He quickly answered. *"You should know that I wouldn't take nobody to the game unless it was you, because you my girl Come on baby, you know I love you! I would never do anything like that to you."*

I wanted to believe him, we were about to get married so why would he jeopardize that? However, I had one more question I had to make sure all my doubt was erased and to have answers to all Lashaun's accusations. *"Well, is she pregnant?"* I asked, hoping that she wasn't. Michael flippantly replied, *"I don't know! Tina is kind of' on the thick side and I wasn't paying attention. Man! Why all the questions, if you don't trust me then we don't need to get married."* A silence fell as I thought about what he said. He was right; trust plays a big part in marriage. And his explanations seemed logical. *"I'm sorry Michael, it's just that Lashaun told me what Princeton said, so I wanted to know the truth."* I could tell he was getting agitated by how he replied, *"Now you have the truth so can we stop talking about this nonsense?"* I felt bad for even questioning him now, if we are to make it in marriage I have to learn not to listen to other people and have faith.

I heard Dad talk about faith all the time in church. *"Without faith it is impossible to please God!"* I guess it was impossible to please people too, since Michael didn't seem to *'pleased'* with me right now. I apologized again and moved on to asking when he was coming to see me. I just wanted to hurry up and get married so that I wouldn't have to listen to all the negativity from people.

Michael came and picked me up the next day and took me to Brundidge and we hung out with Andrea and Mitchell. Michael and Mitchell went to play basketball and Andrea and I went to the mall to hang out. While we were walking through the mall we ran into one of Andrea's friends, Lisa. Andrea introduced me as Michael's fiancé. I noticed that she looked sort of surprised but I figured she was thinking the same thing as everyone else, that we were too young.

During the conversation between the three of us, Lisa mentioned that Tina was pregnant. *"You know Tina is pregnant don't you?"* she said to Andrea. *"Yea, I know she's pregnant and I know who the father is too, she replied.* I'm wondering who this Tina is? Because it was a girl named Tina that Michael said he ran into at the game. And now Tina's name comes up again. I wondered if they were one and the same. Who is Tina, I questioned? Lisa's eyes got big as if she was scared to answer; she quickly looked at Andrea. Andrea simply answered, *"Nobody, just some girl we used to go to school with."*

I knew then that it was the same Tina that Michael had mentioned. I got the impression that Andrea didn't like the girl too much by the expression on her face. *"Oh, because Michael said he ran into her at the football game in Dothan, I replied".* Both Andrea and Lisa now looked shocked but tried to quickly hide their expressions. I didn't know what to think of their reaction but I went on to explain the confusion with my friend's brother believing that Michael was cheating on me with some pregnant girl. I continued to spell out that Michael told me it was Tina who they saw him with, but that he ran into her at the game.

Lisa and Andrea started laughing. I figured they were laughing at the idea of someone assuming that Michael and Tina was an item. Little did I know the joke was on me.

Count down! We are Five days away from getting married I can't wait! I was so excited about getting married that I almost forgot my birthday! My sixteenth birthday was like any other day. Mom and Dad were never big on parties. Now that I think about it, I don't ever remember having a birthday party. ***'Happy Birthday'*** was all I got on the morning of November 11. It really didn't matter to me because I was counting down to November 16, my wedding day! Michael and I were ready to begin our lives together. He was still being the loving and attentive boyfriend he had always been. For my birthday he took me out to eat at the Sizzler and gave me a birthday card with a single rose. Anything that Michael would have given me for my birthday would have been all right with me. Becoming his wife was gift enough for me.

Leading up to my wedding day it seemed the tension in the house dissipated. Dad seemed to have changed his ways and stopped coming into my room. My mom and I even started to bond as mother and daughter. I'll never forget the talk we had on the eve of my wedding day. She told me how that a woman was the person that holds the home together. It is the woman that usually makes the sacrifices. But one thing she said to me that was so heartfelt was, *"And when you have gone as far as you can go and you have nowhere else to go, know that you can always go home."* I don't know what it was about those words that made the tears fall but we both began to cry. I guess she was faced with the reality that her young daughter was rushing into adulthood, and as my mother she knew I was not ready. She was letting me know that regardless of what happens you can always come back. She didn't know that the home she was offering as a place of refuge was the same place I was running away from. Nonetheless, it was an endearing moment between us that I will never forget.

Lashaun called me the night before I was to get married to talk and tell me she was going to miss me, but that she still felt I was making a mistake. She still held to the fact that Michael was cheating on me with Tina. I assured her that he wasn't and that Princeton was mistaken. *"Ok, Yolanda, but I know what I am talking about, but you'll soon find out!" She said.* I was glad that she was concerned about me, but I explained that Michael was not a cheater and that the girl Princeton saw him with was an old school friend. It was no convincing her and I did not want to get into an argument with her; plus I was on our kitchen phone and didn't want my parents to hear the conversation. They had finally accepted the fact that we were getting married. I ended the call by giving her my new number in Brundidge and told her call me anytime.

That night I couldn't sleep in less than twelve hours I was going to be Mrs. Michael Houston! Michael and I were going to the Courthouse in Troy to be married, we planned to be there at 9:00a.m. I already had my outfit picked out. I was wearing a long black A-line skirt with a white ruffled long-sleeved blouse. My shoes were a pair of 3-inch closed toe black pumps. Michael was going to wear some gray baggy pants that fit tight at the ankle (Hammer Pants)with a white button down shirt with some gray Stacey Adam shoes. It seemed the clock was standing still and I couldn't fall asleep. I was anxious to start my new life. I didn't know what was awaiting me in my future but it didn't matter because I was going to prove to everyone that young marriages could work. Love would keep us together!

Finally! The alarm clock went off at 7:30a.m. Normally, I would be getting up to get dressed for school, but it was a different day; I was not going to school. November 16, 1985 was the day of my wedding; it was the day that I was to leave behind years of sorrow, heartache, pain and abuse. And travel to a life filled with love and peace. In just a few hours I would be marrying the man I loved.

I first ironed my skirt and blouse and laid it out on the bed. I then took a long hot shower. I was smiling on the inside and out. I was so very happy. After my shower I dried off and put on my clothes. I took extra time with my hair to make sure it fell in place. But it was not much to do with a Jherri curl, but yet I took my time to make sure every curl was in place. While I was doing my hair I could hear mom in the kitchen preparing breakfast. I realized then that this would be my last breakfast at home.

Michael was to arrive by 8:30a.m so I needed to hurry and eat and be ready when he arrived. One thing Michael didn't like was to be kept waiting. He would really blow his stack if he had to wait or if things didn't go his way.

This was going to be a happy day and I did not want to do anything to make it any different.

Breakfast consisted of scrambled eggs, cheese grits, smoked pork sausage and homemade biscuits. Mom's food was always delectable. Mom, dad and I sat down to eat breakfast; Dad said the grace and we began to eat. Dad made small talk by asking where we were going to live and if Michael was still working. *"We are going to live with Andrea",* I answered in between taking a bite of my sausage. I knew I had already told them that. I purposely ignored the second half of the question. I dare not tell him that Michael had quit his job just a few days ago because he and the manager got into an argument. Michael told me not to worry because he already had put in some more applications for a job and plus he had some money saved up that would hold us over until he got another job. I didn't worry too much about it since we were staying with his sister and because Michael said he had it all planned out. Michael also said that he could get me a job at Burger King working after school.

Me? Working? Now that was scary! I had never worked; had never even thought about it; never had a reason to work. My parents provided well for me and after I started receiving Dad's social security, I didn't want for anything. My mom never worked either; I automatically assumed it would be that way for me too. I was in for a rude awakening because working was not a part of my plan. I was to get married and leave home, continue to go to school and uhm...love Michael. Oh! I was going to work at keeping the bedroom clean that we would sleep in at Andrea's apartment; other than that working was not a part of the plan.

For a fleeting second I thought about changing my mind and staying home but that thought swiftly changed when I remembered the reason I was leaving in the first place. I didn't want to stay at home and continue to deal with my dad and the pressure he brought. I'd just have to hope for the best. Job or no job, I was not passing up the chance to get out of this depressing home.

Michael arrived promptly at 8:30 as planned. He looked so handsome in his outfit that I couldn't stop starring at him. *"You ready to do this?"* he asked as he hugged me. I eagerly nodded my head yes and smiled. *"I am too"* he replied after placing a soft kiss on my lips. Michael spoke to my parents and dad began to badger him by asking him was he sure he wanted to make such a major decision so soon. *"You know marriage is not a game, you can't just quit when you don't want to play anymore,"* dad spoke to him while looking him directly in the eyes. Michael was not moved by his words, he simply replied," *I know, sir"*

"Well, every man has to learn from his own mistakes," dad declared. It was as if he were certain that we wouldn't make it and that we were doomed to fail before we even began. Mom just sat there looking and listening, she never affirmed nor dispelled what dad said. I am sure she felt the same way. But we didn't care because we walked right out that front door and got in Michael's new silver cutlass and drove off to the Brundidge courthouse.

Neither mom nor dad went with us to get married. I'm not sure of the reason why neither of them wanted to go and witness this momentous event, but it didn't matter because I had what I needed to say, *'I do.'* We had the signed parental form, the license and the two main people; Michael and I.

We rode the distance to the courthouse as we talked about what we were going to do afterwards. Michael's mother Daisy was cooking a huge dinner and all of his family would be waiting on us to celebrate our marriage. That's one thing I could say about Michael's family is that they showed support for one another. Though they were somewhat ghettofied they had what I often longed for and that was togetherness. I didn't have that growing up because I was the only child at home and everyone else had gone their separate way. No one bothered to come home much and I guess it was because they didn't want to hear dad's ranting and raving and preaching about how they were living their lives. With Michael's family you could see the love even though they had their bouts of bickering and arguing and cursing each other out. But before the day was out everyone was back laughing and joking as if nothing ever happened. I was going to be a part of a family that welcomed me with open arms. Finally I felt I was a part of something and that I belonged.

Michael and I walked up the twelve steps leading to the courthouse hand in hand. We were silent until we stepped inside the courthouse and asked the receptionist which way to the magistrate's office. She directed us to go down the hall and turn left, the office would be on the right. We followed her directions and entered the Magistrate's office. His secretary was a middle-aged woman with her hair in a bun and wire rimmed glasses that hung off her nose. She looked up as if we were bothering her, "Yes?" she asked in a hoarse sounding voice.

Michael and I both looked at each other; we were reading each other's mind. We both were thinking,' *she is so rude!'* Michael didn't care for white people too much and he didn't mind letting them know. Before he could let his temper get the best of him, I answered, *"We are here to get married."* She looked up at the both of us and shook her head as if to say, I can't believe this. She asked for our paperwork, I gladly gave her everything she asked for. I just wanted her to hurry up before Michael blew his stack. He was already mumbling under his breath because the lady had just rubbed him the wrong way by acting like she didn't want to help us. The secretary processed the paperwork and buzzed the judge. We went into his office and he advised that we had to wait a few moments because we needed another witness. According to state law we had to have two witnesses. The unkind secretary would be a witness and they pulled another lady from one of the other offices to be the second witness.

The judge was a man of short stature with a receding hairline. Basically he didn't have any hair in the middle of his head. I don't know why people keep trying to hold on when the hair is screaming let me go! I mean his hair could have been sideburns. In spite of his balding head he was a nice man. He talked with Michael and I about the ceremony and asked did we have rings; and we did. He talked with us like we were grown folks and didn't belittle us because of our age. I wanted to ask did he marry many teenagers but before I could the secretary and the other witness showed up.

The judge positioned us in front of his desk as the witnesses stood one on each side of us. The whole ceremony took less than ten minutes. I just remember saying, *'I DO'* I guess Michael said it because the next words I remember were, *"I now pronounce you husband and wife and you may salute your bride!"* Now here is the funny part, I have been to a couple of weddings before but had never heard the minister say, *"Salute your bride."* The weddings I went to, the minister said, *"You may now, Kiss your bride."* I guess Michael had never heard *'you may salute your bride'* either because he turned to me and raised his right hand to his forehead as if he were in the army. We both just stood there for a moment and smiled at each other. I was smiling but in my head I was thinking when is the judge going to tell him when to kiss me? Michael and I were anxiously waiting for the next command...to kiss! We did not know that 'Salute' was another way to say kiss your bride.

I soon heard a muffled snicker and quickly turned my head to the judge to see what he was waiting on. When I looked at him his face was as red as a beet as he struggled hard to hold back the laughs. That's when Michael and I both realized that we were looking like dumb idiots! *"Oh! Does that mean I am supposed to kiss her?"* Michael asked as he quickly let his hand fall to his sides. The judge just nodded his head as he was still trying to gain his composure. *"Oh! I thought you were supposed to say, kiss the bride!"* Michael replied as he grabbed me and kissed me!

We didn't need any lessons in kissing; I think we had that down packed. It wasn't our first kiss and it certainly would not be our last kiss but when Michael kissed me this time, I thought my heart was going to burst. It was a short but passionate kiss, it was tender and sweet; it was our first kiss as husband and wife. It was the prelude to the consummation of our marriage.

As soon as we completed our kiss, the judge and the lady that was our second witness exploded into a hearty laugh! *"That was a picture moment,"* she said in her southern drawl. We all chuckled because we knew that she really was speaking of how Michael actually saluted me! So we laughed along with them because it really was funny! The judge congratulated us and wished us the best of luck in our marriage. Both women wished us well also as they walked out the office laughing! I bet we were the butt of their jokes for a day or so. Even still, I will never forget that day it was one of our happiest days!

We left the courthouse as Mr. and Mrs. Houston. I had already practiced signing my name as Mrs. Michael Houston in cursive to see how it would look; and it looked fabulous! As we drove back to my parents house Michael and I swayed to the music playing on the radio and sang to each other. 'You are my lady; you're everything I need and more, by Freddy Jackson. When Michael sang those words to me, I believed he meant them and there was no doubt in my mind that he loved me. Together we would conquer the world.

"So how was it?" Mom asked as we walked through the door smiling. Can't she see it went good? I am smiling and not crying. Geez! And parents think we ask dumb questions. *"We are married!"* I answered. That would let her know that everything went well. *"How does it feel to be a married lady,* she asked nonchalantly. Was this twenty-one questions? I know she meant well but I did not want their questions to turn into a lecture on marriage. We had already heard it all, I didn't want anyone to mess up this feeling I had. I was finally free from the burdens of their stern hand. I was now my own woman; they no longer had shackles on me. I was free! I felt like Martin Luther King, *"Free at last, and free at last! Thank God Almighty, I am FREE at last!!!"*

We sat and talked to mom and dad for a few moments and then packed my luggage and quilts in the car. While Michael and I were outside putting the stuff in the car Lashaun's grandmother, Mrs. Wimble came and gave me another quilt. *"I just wanted to give you something before*

you leave," she said while handing me the quilt. I thanked her for the quilt and placed it in the car. After she walked in the house to speak to my mom and dad, I told Michael, *"What they expect us to do with all these blankets, they want us to smother*
ourselves?" We lived in Alabama and though it was November the weather was still quite nice. Even when it was chilly, I still didn't see the need for all those quilts. I guess it was the thought that counts because it certainly wasn't the money!

After packing the car, we went back in to say our goodbyes and to say that I would see them soon. I hugged and kissed Mom and gave Dad a handshake. I was uncomfortable hugging him or getting too close to him. I would just get this eerie feeling whenever he got too close to me. I didn't know if we would ever have a real daughter & father relationship. The damage he had done was irreparable but yet he was the man that raised me and the only father I knew, strange as it seemed I still loved him. I know it doesn't make sense but that is the way it is.

Mess

The first two months of being married to Michael was great we didn't have a care in the world. Though Michael had not found steady work he did little odd jobs to make money plus we still had a little money that Michael had saved up. Andrea and Mitchell didn't mind us staying with them we went half on the food but they didn't charge us rent. I was scheduled to start school in Brundidge after the New Year. I got my teacher to agree to give me enough homework so that I would not fall behind in my studies and still be able to maintain a passing grade until I started at the new school.

During the day we'd sleep late get up and eat breakfast then lounge around the house and watch T.V. When that became boring to us we would go and visit his mother, hang out in town or either drive down to Troy to visit my parents. I was always happy to go home to visit because I wanted them to see that we were happy and we were making it. Though it had only been a couple of months, I really thought I was proving a point. But Dad burst that bubble one evening we were visiting. *"Yeah, it take about six months for the newness to wear off after that is when the problems begin, he matter- of- factly stated."* I rolled my eyes into the back of my head as I listened to him talk and Mom piggy-backing from what he said. They sound as if I were a car that Michael would get tired after driving me for a while. I certainly hope that wasn't true because we were doing a lot of driving and riding but it wasn't in a car, if you know what I mean. Our lovemaking certainly had not become old. I always looked forward to making love to Michael because each time was better than the last. Whether it was a sweet quickie or a long and passionate session, Michael always set my body on fire. So daddy could keep talking because wasn't nothing getting old as far as Michael and I were concerned. I was enjoying this newfound freedom and I was happy with being married to Michael; everything was lovely! Little did I know that trouble was on the horizon.

I'll never forget the Wednesday afternoon that my world began to take a spiral turn. Wednesday was the day that Michael would take his mom to the Green Spot over in Banks, Alabama. Green Spot was a small discount grocery store and on Wednesdays they would have a sale on all their meat. Everyone in the surrounding areas would drive to Banks to get meat.

Michael had left to take Daisy to the store and I had stayed at the house with Andrea. Mitchell was still at work. We were sitting there watching TV when the phone rang. Andrea answered the phone and it was a brief conversation. *"He's not here right now, oh really! I'm not sure when he'll be back; I'll tell him when he returns. Ok. Bye."* And that was the end of the conversation. I didn't think much about the conversation, just figured it was someone calling for Mitchell. Andrea returned to the living room and flopped back on the pea green sofa she was sitting on and continued to watch T.V.

About an hour later Michael and Mitchell walked through the door. Mitchell had just gotten off from work and Michael had already dropped Daisy off at home. Michael came over and gave me a kiss on the cheek and sat down next to me and we curled up to continue watching T.V.

Mitchell and Andrea went into their bedroom, soon Mitchell opened the door and yelled for Michael to come here. As Michael walked to the bedroom I was wondering what was so important that they couldn't say it in front of me? Once Michael walked into the bedroom they closed the door. I could hear their voices but couldn't make out what they were saying. Whatever they were saying, sounded as if Michael was not happy.

When he opened the door, I heard Andrea loudly say, "you betta' tell her or I will, because you can't hide the truth anymore!" By this time I am walking down the hallway to meet Michael because obviously something is wrong. As we met in the hallway, I could tell by the look on Michael's face that he is angry. Before I can say anything he says, "Let's go!" as he places his hand on my shoulder to direct me to turn around. *"No! we're not going anywhere, what is it that you need to tell me?"* I curiously ask, as I back up against the wall. I wanted to know what was going on. "Yolanda, I said let's go!" He screams at me. By now I am getting mad because first he hollering at me and second I know something is going on and I wasn't going anywhere until he told me what was up! *"After you tell me what is going on then we can go"!* I yelled back as I started back towards Andrea's room. As I turned my back on Michael he grabbed me and pushed me up against the wall and slapped me. *"Yolanda, this is not the time to push my buttons, now I said let's go!"* and he continues to grab me by my arm and pulls me towards the front door.

I experienced shock, anger and pain all in one instance. I could not believe he had just hit me. I am holding my face because I'm feeling the sting of the slap. I could feel the side of my right eye swelling and the tears began to fall. He had never done anything like this before so I know he had to be really angry about whatever Andrea said to him; otherwise I know he would never have hit me. I should have just gone ahead and got in the car, I thought to myself as we reached the door.

Mitchell and Andrea heard the commotion and came out to see what was going on. *"Aye, man everything ok out here?* Mitchell asked, just as we had stepped out the front door. I went ahead and walked to the car so he or Andrea couldn't see my face. Michael and Mitchell talked for a few moments. I heard Mitchell tell Michael to handle his business and Michael replied that he had everything in control.

When Michael got in the car I just looked at him and rolled my eyes at him and then just looked straight ahead. I didn't know what to say to him. It was a lot going on and I seemed to be the only person that didn't know what was going on. *"Baby, I am sorry that I hit you, I really didn't mean to do it, but I was mad and you weren't listening to me."* He said as he rubbed the left side of my face. I'm thinking joker you rubbing the wrong side, you hit me on the right side. Didn't he see the whelp on the side of my eye? Anyway he just had better been glad that I loved him because everybody knows I did not like anybody touching my face. I didn't even like it when my mom used to stick her finger in my face. I would get heated when she did that but I knew I couldn't fight her. I treasured my life no matter how distraught it was sometime.

I looked at Michael as he spoke to me and I could see the hurt in his eyes as he looked at me and I knew he did not mean to hit me. *"Baby, I forgive you but what is going on? What was Andrea talking about? What is it that you need to tell me?* I asked him. I really couldn't think of what was so bad that he was mad at his sister. He and Andrea were very close but I knew whatever it was I was not going to want to hear it. I could just tell from how hesitant Michael was. Michael looked straight ahead as he drove down the street. The next words I heard out of his mouth were unbelievable. I literally thought that I was in the middle of a horrible dream, a nightmare!

"I have a baby on the way." Michael said ever so calmly. I looked at Michael and then looked at my stomach because if he had said what I thought he said, then I should have a bulge in my midsection. *"What do you mean you have a BABY ..On ..The ..Way? And what Stork is sending him because I am not pregnant!"* I yelled in between gasping for breath. I was about to be hysterical! I could not believe what I was hearing. *"Girl, first of all you going to stop yelling like you ain't got no sense, and second of all I wanted to tell you but I knew you would leave me if I did"* he replied in an elevated voice. The audacity of him to tell me to stop yelling when he just dropped a bombshell on me! He probably right I may

have left him but he didn't give me the opportunity to see if that was true, but then again I may not have because I loved him. A wave of thoughts went through my mind, I couldn't think about possibilities of the past I had to think about the realities of the present. My man had gotten somebody pregnant other than me.

Michael went on to explain that Tina the girl that he claimed was just an old friend was pregnant. Oh! You think that is something; what about he tells me that he has another son by her! His son is two years old. Michael George Houston, Jr. I was about to lose my mind. The words of my dad kept ringing in my ear, *"those Houston's ain't no good."* He was talking about the granddaddy but it seemed it was applying to the grandchild too. I was screaming and hollering and crying so much so that I had not paid attention to where Michael was driving. When I realized that we had just parked at the hospital, I calmed down long enough to ask why we were at the hospital.

"Didn't you hear me say that I had a baby on the way?" Michael answered nonchalantly. During the whole time of him telling me about the child and that Tina was pregnant he had acted as if it were no big deal. I was the one that was in a frenzy! I had heard him say he had a baby on the way, but I didn't know he meant that the baby was actually on the way as we spoke. Tina was in labor. It was

Tina that Andrea had talked to earlier in the day. She had called asking for Michael to tell him she was in labor. I had thought the call was for Mitchell.

While Michael apologized to me about not being truthful he gave no other explanation as to why he lied and didn't tell me that he had a child in the beginning. Or as to why he lied about Tina being pregnant. He basically, told me that I had to accept the reality of him having a child and that he was about to be a daddy again for a second time. He even went as far as to say that I was his wife and that wives support their husbands. *"For better or worse. You remember you said that when you married me, right?"* What could I say? I did say for better or worse. Not knowing that my worse would begin 6 months after saying 'I do'.

I had to walk in that hospital and sit in the waiting room while, my husband went into the labor room with his ex-girlfriend. I felt so humiliated, the man that I loved and thought would never do anything to hurt me had just stuck a knife through my heart more than once in one day. I wanted to die. As I sat there and thought about the events of the day, I was reminded of a truism that my mom used to say, *'You made your bed now lie in it.'* Therefore, it was nothing for me to do but to deal with the problems in my life. I certainly was not going to call and tell my parents what had happened because they were just going to say," *I told you so."*

Tina had another little boy and named him Andrew. Michael came out of the delivery room all happy like he was the proud father. He even asked me did I want to go see him. Heck! No! I didn't want to go see him. And I was not mad at the baby. I was mad because I was the wife. I should have been the one to have his baby. I wondered why no one bothered to tell me of Michael's secrets. I guess blood really is thicker than water because no one gave a hint that he had a child. I thought about the times we were trying to get pregnant so we could have a reason to get married, not knowing that he already had a baby. I had imagined many times how it would be the day I told him I was pregnant and seeing his reaction. I should be the one that gave him his namesake, not the ex-girlfriend! She was the *'EX'* for a reason so how was it that I felt like the *"EX"*?

I would like to tell you that the baby was the end of our problems, but it is not true. Tina didn't cause us a lot of problems concerning the baby but she didn't hide in a closet either. Once upon a time she was just a rumor to me, but now she was around all the time. She was like an old piece of furniture that you wanted to get rid of but you still had some use for it. I eventually got used to the fact that she was around even though I didn't like it.

Michael and I both got jobs. He got a job at one of the factories in town and I went to work at one of the fast food restaurants. We wanted to move out of Andrea and Mitchell's apartment and get our own. We actually found an apartment in the same complex. Just as it seemed our life was smoothing out, trouble began again, this time with the beatings from Michael. He would just go off on me for no apparent reason. He began to treat me more like his child than his wife. Little by little his attitude became more intense. I could never figure out what would cause his flare ups.

I remember once, he blacked my eye because I said I didn't want to go over his mother's house. I had just gotten off from work and I was tired. He wanted to go over his mom's place where everybody was hanging out. I told him I wasn't going. Big mistake! The next thing I know his fist was in my eye and I was lying in the floor. He simply walked out the door. He later came back and wanted to have sex as if nothing had happened. He made no reference to my swollen and black eye. I was too scared to turn him down for sex because I didn't want to get beat again. I also remember what happened when I said no to my dad when he wanted sex. Therefore, *'No'* was not an option when it related to sex.

Another time, I came home from work and saw Jherri curl stain on my pillowcase.. I knew it wasn't mine because I had grown out of the curl and my hair was now permed. When I asked him about it, he hit me so hard I saw the stars and the moon! I was able to swing back and hit him in the face. Why did I do that? He beat me like I was his childhood rival. He hit me with a 2x4 piece of wood that we used to support our mattress. The blow landed on the middle of my back. It's a miracle that he didn't break my back. I remember using my hands to protect my head from the blows. I was screaming, *"Michael! Stop! Please stop!"* He finally did but he made sure to tell me not to be accusing him of anything! That was the end of that conversation. I knew he was cheating and there was only one person that I knew had a Jherri curl...Tina. I had no proof but I felt he was still messing with her. It took days for my bruises to heal. Michael along with everybody else would always pretend they did not see the black eyes and the bruises. Pretending I was good at but I couldn't pretend I wasn't getting beat; it was too obvious.

On one occasion we went to visit my parents and at this point I had not told them about the issues Michael and I were having. But I thought if I told my mom that maybe that would make him stop. I could not have been so wrong. I told my mom and she was furious! She told him that she did not let me marry him for him to be beating on me. And that she had better not hear of him hitting me again! Michael listened and said, *"Yes, maam, I'm sorry."* I can't remember where my dad was at the time and why he didn't say anything, but anyway I thought it would be all over. As we drove back to Brundidge, Michael was silent all the way home. I didn't know if he was mad or embarrassed that I had told my mom. So I was nervous, because his silence wasn't a good thing.

We went to visit his mom, Daisy. Daisy's house was like the hang out spot, it's where everybody kind of' hung out and partied. We were sitting on the couch and out of nowhere and in front of everybody there; he hauled off and punched me on the side of my head. Nobody said a word except for Daisy and she only said, *"You shouldn't be hitting on that girl like that, how would you like it if someone did you like that?"* He never paid her any attention as he pulled me up from the couch and pushed me towards the bathroom, which was in the back of the house. After we reached the bathroom, he rammed my head in the window. The window shattered, luckily no glass got in my hair. I remember crying and screaming, hoping that would make him stop. It didn't work; the tears didn't affect him anymore. He had locked the bathroom door so whoever was banging on the door couldn't get in. *"You thought I wasn't going to say anything about you telling your mother about me hitting you! You don't be telling anybody anything about what goes on with us! Do you hear me?"* he yelled as he pointed his finger in my face. I simply hung my head down and whimpered," *Yes".* He then punched me in my face again as if to make his point.

How could this be happening to me? Why is my life filled with so much pain? I wondered to myself as Michael continued to yell at me to clean up my face and the glass. He had such a way of humiliating me. I thought I had left a home where I was humiliated and abused. But I didn't do anything but change addresses. Michael had turned in to Dr. Jekyll and Mr. Hyde. I had to walk on eggshells because I didn't know what was going to tee him off.

When Michael finished what he had to say he opened the door to an unexpected surprise. A guy named Alexander that usually hung out at Daisy's house was standing at the bathroom door when Michael opened the door. Alexander pushed Michael against the wall and told him, *"You want to hit somebody? Why don't you hit me, hit me! I'm a man and you a man, so act like one and hit me!"* I was surprised and scared at the same time because I didn't want them fighting and because although

Alexander was trying to help he was making matters worse. He didn't know that's why I just got my tail beat because my mother had tried to intervene. Michael didn't take well to people getting in his business so I knew they were about to go at it.

To my surprise Michael didn't raise a fist or finger to Alexander. He simply said, *"Man, I ain't got no beef with you. I was just puttin' my ole lady in check."* He was so composed as if he had not just finished beating my tail. I couldn't believe that he wasn't all up in Alexander's face and ready to bounce on him for butting in his business.

Alexander stood about 6'1 and had a medium solid build to him. Although he was taller and bigger than Michael, I still didn't see Michael backing down out of a fight with him because of size. *"Yeah, just what I thought, you a punk ass nigga'. You get off beating up on a lady but you're not man enough to fight a man. Don't ever put your hands on her again while you are in my presence. Whatever else you do is your business and if she choose to stay and let you use her for a punching bag is her business, but don't do that shit in my presence!"* Alexander exclaimed. Again, to my astonishment, Michael, humbly replied, *"Like I said man, I don't have no problems with you."* And then he walked off back into the living room.

I continued to pick up the broken window glass as I listened to Daisy proclaim," *you all going to pay for that window!"* Alexander peeked his head into the doorway and asked if I were ok? I didn't even look up as I answered him and stated that I was ok. But I really wasn't. I thought he would walk away after I answered him but he didn't. He entered into the bathroom and knelt down beside me, out of the corner of my eye I saw his hands coming for my face and I flinched and my arm automatically went up to guard my face.

Alexander quickly pulled back and said in a caring voice, *"Yolanda, you don't have to be scared of me, I would never hit or hurt you. I was just trying to wipe the tears from your face. And you should not allow anyone too mistreat you like Michael has. You deserve better but if you don't know that then I feel sorry for you."* His words made the tears start to flow again because I wasn't so sure I deserved better. I felt I deserved it because it was payback for my sins and wrongdoing. After all, that's what dad used to say, *'The wages of sin is death!'* Dying is what I felt like doing; at least if I were dead I would have no pain.

Alexander helped me pick up the remaining pieces of glass and left me alone to clean my face. As I looked in the mirror at my bruised face, I wondered how I could get

Michael to stop beating me and love me like a husband should; wishful thinking.

Things between us were bad in every way. We had fallen behind in the rent and they were threatening to put us out. All we had for food was bread and Vienna sausages because after trying to pay part of the bills we didn't have enough money for food. I didn't like Vienna sausages so I ate a lot of toast.

The lowest of lows came when we were on a food hunt and we had stopped at Andrea's house. They had left their left over scraps on the kitchen table in the Styrofoam carry out plates. As soon as Andrea was out of sight we rummaged through the scraps trying to get a morsel of food. I felt like a homeless person and a thief at the same time. A homeless person usually doesn't know where his next meal was coming from; we didn't either and we were one step away from being homeless. I felt like a thief because we were sneaking and taking somebody else's scraps. I had never felt so low in my life.

Michael refused to tell anybody how bad off we were because of his pride. He was still trying to maintain his image. If I couldn't sneak food home from work, I knew that would cost me a beating. We would get one free meal a day at work. I just started bagging my food and taking it home just so Michael could have something to eat. Once when I came home without food we got into a fight. I was tired and was not in the mood for the drama. He hit me in my face again and I got mad and swung back instead of trying to protect myself. Why did I do that? I knew from before that if I tried to fight him back it would only make him madder. I was right; Michael beat me that night so much that he took me to the hospital himself.

On the way to the hospital he told me to tell the doctor I fell down a flight of stairs. Little did he know I was already planning on telling them that he had beaten me up. The nurse called my name and Michael remained in the waiting area. The nurse was going through her regular triage but she was looking at me with a concerned look on her face. *"Who did this to you honey",* she asked while taking my temperature. I paused for just a moment as I thought one last time what I was about to do. But I had had enough of Michael's insane behavior; I wanted a way to escape. *"The person that did this to me, is in the waiting room,"* I whispered. Where we were sitting you could look through a glass window into the waiting room. I looked out into the waiting room and described Michael to her, but was careful not to point in his direction. I don't remember the nurse's name but I remember her face. She was an older lady about fifty years old, looked like she had a tan with blonde permed hair, meaning it was curly and frizzy. I always thought it funny how a perm for black people straightens the natural curl of our hair, but a perm for a white person adds curl to their naturally straight hair. But anyway, she also had an old scar over her left eye that looked like she had been deeply cut but it may not have healed properly. Once she had made out who Michael was she lovingly touched my hand and told me not to worry that I would be safe.

She took me to one of the little examining rooms in the back. The next thing I knew two police were entering the room. They asked me some questions about what had happened and I explained to them how Michael had beaten me because I had not brought food home from work. After getting all the information, they explained that after the doctor examined me they would arrest Michael for assault and battery charges. I guess Michael may have seen the police somehow because the police later came back and said he had left the premises.

I ended up having a sprained arm and a lot of bruises and contusions and two black eyes. The officers asked me did I want to proceed with pressing charges. I said no, but if they could take me to a friend's house I would be all right. I had the officer drop me off at Delores and Jimmy's house. I knew their house was the last place that Michael would look for me. Jimmy and Delores were a young white couple that lived around the corner from where Michael and I lived. Jimmy actually used to work with Michael while he was still at the factory. Delores and I had become friends because we had some things in common. She was 17 years old with a baby and she and Jimmy had been married for a year.

I knew he wouldn't look for me there and he probably wouldn't be anywhere near our home if he suspected the police were after him. The next day Delores drove me to Troy to my parents' house. Both my mom and dad were in shock and angered over how I looked. I know I looked like a run over raccoon with my blackened eyes and swollen lip. My mom was ranting and raving about Michael beating me up. *"I told that boy never to put his hands on you again! You just wait until I see him,"* she stated through gritted teeth! I don't know what she thought she was going to do, but the fact that she was mad let me know she loved me. I actually had never seen my mom so angry except when she was mad at Michael for beating me. I could tell that my dad was upset about it but he didn't say much except, "I knew them Houston's were no good!"

The next morning I had dad drive me to Brundidge to my apartment to get my clothes. Michael must have still been hiding out because fortunately for me he was not at home. I quickly got my things and left. I had one last paycheck due me from Quick Burger. Dad drove me to pick it up and I let them know I would not be back. It didn't take long for Michael to realize that I had gone back home to my parents' house. He soon started calling and apologizing and telling me he missed me. Truth was I missed him too; I wanted to believe that he would not do it again but I could not be sure.

About a month after I had left Michael he came to visit me, he said we needed to talk. I knew I missed Michael but when I saw him all the feelings I had for him came flooding back. I ran straight into his arms. Michael missed me just as much because he grabbed me up off the ground and swung me around and kissed me long and hard. It seemed like old times. Michael and I took a long drive and just talked. He kept apologizing for all the things he did to me. He went on to explain that he realized he needed me in his life when I left him.

During our talk I began to understand why Michael treated me the way he did. He said he and his father were never close and he never had a man around to show him how to treat a woman. His dad and Daisey fought all the time. And Daisey had men come in and out of her life after she broke up with his dad. Although Daisy was free spirited she seemed to attract the men that abused and mistreated her too. On several occasions Michael and Mitchell had to go intervene when she and her male friends would get into a fight. Therefore, fighting and arguing were the only way he knew how to deal with women.

I understood his point of view but it did not make it right. I explained to him, *"I love you but I don't want to be your personal punching bag. You have to find a way to keep your anger under control."* Michael promised he would work on it if I would come back to him. He claimed he couldn't make it without me. He sounded convincing but I was not going to take the bait that easily. I asked him about Tina and if he were still messing around with her. He said no and that nothing happened since we been married. Michael claimed that it had only been a one-time thing after we started dating. He admits that he made a mistake and sorry that he did it. But the fact remains that he has two kids with her and she will always be a part of his life because of the kids. That was a hard pill to swallow, but I understood. I believed him. He wouldn't have come all the way to Troy to tell me that if he didn't love me. He could have continued on with his life without me, there was nothing connecting us together; we didn't have any children therefore, it had to be love.

We were so engrossed in conversation that we drove all the way to Dothan, Alabama. We decided to get a hotel room so that we could have some privacy. Although we were still married I didn't feel comfortable with Michael sleeping in my old room at my parents house; besides I knew mom and dad were still upset over what Michael had did to me. I asked Michael why had he left the hospital. Just as I had assumed, he said he saw the police and figured I had told them that he had jumped on me. I explained that it was actually the nurse that had called the police and that I had refused to press charges. That was partially true, the nurse did call the police but I didn't feel it important for him to know that I actually told the nurse that he had beat me.

Michael and I rekindled our love that night inside the unfashionable motel. We made love like it was no tomorrow. Michael was so passionate; he looked into my eyes as if he were looking at me for the first time. He took his time and kissed every part of my body as if he had found a golden treasure. The coolness of his lips ignited a fire within me and caused my juices to flow. I begged for him to reconnect us and join our bodies together as one. I wanted to feel him inside me and extinguish the fire that he had ignited. When we finally came together as one, we found each other's rhythm and swayed and rocked until we both exploded together. And just when I thought it was over, Michael came back for more and took me to a higher plateau than before. It was electrifying and exhilarating! When we finished I was exhausted and we fell asleep with our bodies entangled.

The morning after, we showered together and went and ate breakfast at Waffle House. Michael assumed that after a passion filled night that I would be going back to Brundidge with him. *"So baby, what do you think your parents will say when you tell them you moving back home*?" he asked while chewing on a piece of sausage. I really hadn't made up my mind if I were going back to him or not. Yes! I was elated that we had talked and the previous night was wonderful but I was not sure that things would be different if we moved back together.

"I'm not sure I am going back to Brundidge yet," I answered while playing with the overcooked scrambled eggs and cheese that were on my plate. Michael looked stunned. I went on to ask him what guarantee he could give me that things wouldn't go back to the way they were before. *"Baby, I thought we talked about this last night. I promised you that I would work on my temper, I don't know what else you want me to say,"* he replied while looking sincerely into my eyes. While waiting for my response he reached across the table and grabbed my hands and as he continued to stare into my eyes he told

me that everybody deserves a second chance and he was begging me to give him one.

I understood that people were deserving of second chances but I still was not sure. My heart and my body was saying go back. But my mind was saying, No! My final answer to Michael was to give me more time to figure out what I wanted to do. I had to be sure that things were going to be different. I didn't want to go back to the chaos, I had to be sure I wouldn't have to be digging through other people's left-overs for food, and my body couldn't take any more hits and punches. I just simply needed more time to make a decision. My parents were the least of my worries; I was more worried about him keeping his promises. And to tell the truth of the matter, being back home was not so bad. Dad hadn't tried to mess with me, the church folk had stopped shaking their head at me when I walked in church as if I were a disgrace to my family and mom and I were having adult conversations. Not to mention, I wasn't getting knocked upside my head and let me add there was plenty of food. So Michael would just have to give me more time.

To my surprise he humbly agreed. He stated he was aware of the problems he caused and he would do anything to get me back. After that day Michael continued to come over on the weekends and it was if we were dating all over again. Sometimes I would even go to Brundidge and stay the weekend with him. Everything was going fine with us, but what Michael didn't know was that in between his visits on the weekends I was spending a lot of time next door at my friend LaShaun's house, but it wasn't LaShaun that I was spending time with, it was her brother Princeton.

Princeton was the one that had told me that Michael was cheating on me before I got married. He and Lashaun and I were always cool with each other. Their dad was a preacher also so I could always go to their house when I couldn't go anywhere else. Upon coming back home I would go over and watch television with them. Strangely enough, they never asked me anything about Michael or why I was back home. We just picked up from where we left off.

One Saturday evening, I called to see what they were up too and Princeton answered the phone. He told me that LaShaun was not home she had gone out on a date. I told him that I was just calling to see what they were up too. He said he was watching a movie he had rented and that I could come over and watch it with him if I wanted too. Since I wasn't doing anything I told him I would.

In less than five minutes I was knocking at their front door. Princeton came to the door with an orange and white football shirt on and some black shorts. He looked so cute. Princeton probably was about 5'9 with a stocky build. His skin was chocolate brown and though he had the teenage acne he was still a handsome guy. I loved to look in his eyes because they were big and bright but something about them seemed to always hold my attention and when he laughed it was contagious. Everyone around him would begin to laugh whenever they heard him laugh because it was such an enthusiastic laugh.

Princeton let me in and we went into the den where we would normally watch T.V. His parents were home but they were upstairs in their bedroom. The rule of their house was that they could have company of the opposite sex but they could never take anyone into their rooms. And since all the bedrooms were upstairs they didn't worry about the company being in the den. Of course they didn't worry about me being there anyway because I was over there so much even before I got married. They considered me as part of the family.

Princeton was watching some horror movie, I don't remember the name of the movie but I do remember him starting the movie over so we could watch it from the beginning. I sat on one end of the couch and he sat somewhat in the middle. He was close but not that close, actually another person could have sat between us. We began watching the movie in silence but me being the inquisitive person that I am began asking questions about what was going to happen before it happened. *"Is she going to get killed? Why is he chasing her?"* Princeton started off answering my questions and before long the conversation extended into something else. Soon we were so engrossed in conversation that we had forgotten about the movie. Princeton was easy to talk to and he put my mind at ease. I didn't think about Michael when I was around him and tonight was no different.

We had talked so much we both were thirsty. Princeton went into the kitchen to get us something to drink. He came back with two glasses of grape Kool-Aid. After setting the glasses on the glass table Princeton sat closer to me; close enough for him to put his arm around me. I didn't say anything nor did I move over, I just took a deep breath and exhaled. *"What's wrong?"* he asked. I immediately replied, *"Nothing!"* I did not want him to know that I was nervous. Maybe he sensed my nervousness because before I could say anything else he leaned over and kissed me. It was a quick kiss without any tongue.

Princeton pulled back and looked at me to see what my response was. I bashfully smiled and looked away. Princeton then pulled me towards him and leaned in and kissed me again, and this time I kissed him back. Princeton gently pushed me back until my head was resting on the armrest of the couch. I was halfway sitting and half way lying on the couch. Princeton comfortably positioned himself on me and we continued to passionately kiss.

We continued to kiss until we heard footsteps and saw the kitchen light come on. We quickly stopped kissing and repositioned ourselves on the couch. Luckily, you couldn't see into the den from the kitchen but the footsteps were hastily approaching. It ended up being Princeton's dad coming down to get a snack. He peeped into the den to see what Princeton was doing. He saw us there watching the movie. He spoke and asked how I was doing and asked what we were watching.

Princeton quickly explained what the movie was about. After a few moments of small talk his dad reminded us both that the next day was Sunday and then he retreated back upstairs.

I took that as my signal to go home. After all it was almost midnight so I told Princeton I had to leave. He told me I didn't have to leave yet and that I should stay until LaShaun got home. I told him I had to go because I didn't want dad to lock the doors on me. That was partially true but truth of the matter was I wanted to put some distance between us. The interruption gave me time to come to my senses and remember that I was still married although we were separated. But the fact remained I belonged to someone else and Michael and I were trying to patch things up.

Princeton walked me to the door and I gave him a hug and walked back across the yard to my house. I couldn't help but smile thinking about what had transpired between us. It felt nice spending time with Princeton, I always knew we were attracted to each other I just wondered why it took so long for him to say anything. Truthfully, he hadn't said anything, but the kiss said it all.

For the next three months I enjoyed the company of both Princeton and Michael. Michael continued to visit every other weekend and in between I visited Princeton on a regular basis. Princeton and I fought hard to try and remain just friends but the chemistry between us overruled our desire to do what was right. The passionate kisses, lingering hugs and gentle touches soon led to many explosive love-making sessions.

While I knew what we were doing was wrong Princeton had become like a drug, I simply couldn't get enough of him. He gave me the attention that I sometimes felt I was not receiving from Michael. Princeton craved for me just as much as I craved for him. He was easy to be with but it was more than just sex, he listened to me. Our conversations were stimulating and I could be myself with him. I didn't have to walk on egg shells; I could relax and enjoy the moment. We clicked.

With Michael I was just his prize possession he didn't want to lose. Truth is I didn't want to lose him either, he was my husband but Princeton was my lover and friend. I didn't want to let either one of them go but I knew a choice had to be made. The guilt was eating me up on the inside. I couldn't look Michael in the eyes for fear he'd recognize what I had been doing. Part of me felt justified for the many times that Michael had cheated on me, but the other side said, *'two wrongs don't make a right.'*

Though it was hard to do, I eventually decided to go back with Michael. Needless to say, Princeton didn't take it too well. *"How are you going back to him, after everything he's done to you? "*Princeton asked as he glared at me. *"He's my husband!* I replied, *I'm obligated to try and make it work." No, you're obligated to be happy,* he yelled back! *And you know he is not going to make you happy"*

The sad part was that deep down I knew that Princeton was right. However, I still loved Michael and I still hoped that we could make it work. After all, marriage was not just about being happy it was about finding ways to make it last forever; hoping in the long run that happiness is a part of your life.

Princeton's eyes pleaded with me not to go as I backed out the door. I slowly backed away as I kept my eyes on him. I wanted to have a visual of him for as long as I could because once I left I knew there was no turning back. *"I'm sorry,"* is all I could get out as I finally made it out the door. Princeton didn't say a word but I could see the pain in his eyes. I turned and walked back to my parent's house as quickly as I could with tears in my eyes. I hoped that my decision wouldn't come back to later haunt me, but for now I had made my choice.

Needless to say my parents thought I was being a fool. The only person happy about my decision was Michael. As soon as I had called him and told him I wanted to come back he was elated. The next day he came and picked me up and we headed back to Brundidge to begin our life together for the second time or third……I'd lost count, but we started over again!

Michael and I started over and everything was perfect. Sorry, but that is not the truth. As usual the first couple of weeks were lovely! Michael was so loving and attentive just like when we first met. We both had jobs and it seemed we were finally becoming a young happy family.

Funny how things can swiftly change, well maybe it wasn't all so swiftly. Maybe it all changed in front of my eyes and I failed to see it. I could go on and on about maybe's and what if's, but the reality was that our happy life had taken a turn for the worse....again!

Tina was constantly hanging around with the babies; of course that was a constant reminder of Michael's infidelities. But what was I to say these were his children and he had every right to see them. It seemed to me that Tina and Michael were a bit chummier than they should be. When I would question Michael about it, he would just say I was imagining things; and to deal with the fact that she was his children's mother. As hurtful as it was, it was a truth I could not deny!

I had my suspicions but I never followed Michael or tried to set him up in order to learn the truth. I merely continued to hope and believe that what I was feeling was not true. It was like, I knew he was guilty of something but

I didn't have the evidence to prove it. My mother used to always say, *"Never go looking for trouble because trouble will always find you."* Little did I know how that cliché would become a true statement in my life.

Michael and I worked the same hours but since he drove and I didn't he would drop me off and pick me up from work. One day, the manager sent me and a coworker Mercedes home early because too many people were scheduled to work that day. Mercedes agreed to take me home because she stated I didn't live far from the day care where she had to pick up her daughter.

I had her stop me by the grocery store so I could get a few groceries for dinner. I planned on surprising Michael with his favorite meal: Meatloaf, corn on the cob and rice. Once I got home, I was going to call his job and leave a message for him that he didn't have to pick me up from work.

Imagine my surprise when I arrived home and Michael's car was in the driveway. I knew he had to work because when we left home and he was in his uniform, plus the T-shirt factory he worked at never closed. Therefore I thought maybe he got sick at work and came home. I was so about to find out how far from the truth that was.

I opened the door and entered our small living room. The first thing I noticed was the purse sitting on the coffee table. Well since I had my purse on my shoulder I knew immediately it wasn't mine. My blood immediately started to boil because this boy had somebody up in my house! And the sad thing was they were so engrossed in what they were doing they didn't even hear me come in.

I sat the groceries on the kitchen table and headed down the hallway that led to our bedroom. The hallway was very small but it seemed like it was a mile long that day. I didn't know what I was going to do once I reached the bedroom but I just know I was madder than a raging bull! Everything was going thru my mind in the ten seconds it took to reach the bedroom door. I slung open the door and there they were; Michael and Tina naked and tangled up together sleep.

When I slung the door open, I startled both of them. Without thought I grabbed the nunchucks that Michael kept on the dresser and went to swinging! Michael still in a daze looked like he had seen a ghost all while trying to block the blows from the sticks. Tina with her trifling behind pulled the covers up over her body as if that would protect her from the blows. I was swinging with every ounce of power and anger I had in me. I don't know how many blows I got in before I felt Michael's fist connect with my right jaw. The force from the blow rattled my already clenched teeth and sent me reeling to the floor.

Michael was on top of me and had me pinned to the floor as he punched me again in my face. The nunchucks were pinned between us so I had no weapon to fight back with or to use for protection. He was screaming, *"Are you crazy? Calm the f*#@ down!"* I was still trying to maneuver myself to get out from under him and to try to grab the nunchucks. Though I was physically hurt I was still angry and still had some fight in me. I wanted to kill him.

I calmed down long enough to allow him to get off of me. When he did the nunchucks slid off my body to the floor. Michael stepped away to glance in the mirror to check out the knot that was building on his forehead. When he did I quickly grabbed the nunchucks and took one more swing at him and the stick landed across his nose and blood spewed out. I dropped the sticks and bolted for the bedroom door. I knew he was going to kill me.

As I reached the bedroom door, I saw Tina out of the corner of my eye. She had somehow in the midst of the confusion managed to get her clothes on but was backed in a corner looking like she was afraid to move. I made it partly down the hallway before Michael reached me and yanked me by my hair and slung me against the wall face first. Before I could blink I felt those same nunchucks that I had just used as a weapon come across my back. I crumpled to the floor again this time using my hands as protection to cover my head from the blows of the sticks. With Michael being a black belt in karate he could have easily killed me.

Ironically, it was Tina's screams that stopped him from continuing to hit me with those nunchucks. When I saw the look in his eyes when I caused his nose to bleed, I knew I was in big trouble. Sad to say, I was grateful she was there because that day could have been the last day of my life. As I lay sprawled in the middle of the hallway, this man that I called my husband, the man I had a love-hate relationship; gently pushed me out of the way with his foot as if I were a piece of trash and proceeded to leave with his mistress. He had the audacity to yell back before exiting the house, *"You better hope my nose is not broke or else you'll have hell to pay!"*

I just lie there on the floor with a wave of emotions tunneling thru me. Pain, hurt, resentment, anger, disappointment, you name it I felt it that day. How did I end up here in this situation? All I wanted was to love the man I married and try and make my marriage work. Didn't this same man for months pursue me and coax me back into his arms? Did he not tell me that he loved me and that he had changed? Why then would you risk it all? Why am I the beaten wife lying in a disheveled mess? Why? Why? Why? Why did I leave one home of misery only to move into another one? Why did it seem my life never had any happiness? Why was I even born; because at that very moment I wanted to die.

I don't know how long I lie there on the floor drowning in my misery. I must have fell asleep there because the next thing I remember was hearing Michael's voice, *"Yolanda, wake up are you ok?"* he asked as he rubbed my forehead. I was startled as I opened my eyes and saw his bandaged nose. I jerked my head and tried to sit up but when I did, I yelled in pain. I felt as if every bone in my body was broken. Michael acted as if he were my knight and shining armor as he helped me get up. We slowly walked to the bedroom and I sat on the rumpled bed. The bed he had been in earlier with Tina.

Michael was tenderly, checking me over for bruises and asking was I ok. I couldn't believe my ears. Had I been dreaming? Had we been robbed and beaten; or was this not the man that had caused me all this pain both physically and emotionally. This was a prime example of how Michael would switch from being the doting and loving husband to the mean and cruel abuser and back to the attentive man he was being at that very moment. Talk about confusion.

Don't you know that all this man could say after all that had just happened hours earlier was that he was sorry. *"I didn't mean to hurt you, but when you hit me with those nunchucks I snapped!"* So now this was my fault? He gave no explanation about the affair and I didn't ask, because at that moment I didn't care. I was planning my final exit strategy. I had had enough! I was not going to play the fool anymore.

I allowed Michael to think that I was the dumb forgiving wife as before and that we would just forget everything that had happened. Michael's nose was broken the doctor reset it and bandaged it up. He said the doctor told him it would heal and gave him some pain meds.

The next morning, Michael felt well enough to go to work, I didn't, plus my right jaw was swollen. I told Michael that I would just stay home and put some ice on my face to get the swelling down and because I didn't feel like answering questions from my coworkers. All this was partly true. Michael fell for the okey- doke and left for work.

Little did he know, I had planned to leave. I only had to hope that everything would go as planned. When I finally got up to put my plan in action, I was a little dizzy and queasy, not to mention my body was so sore. I was slow moving. Every step I made was full of pain. I remembered that I had not eaten anything since lunch time the day before. I entered the kitchen and realized the bag of groceries I had purchased to fix Michael's favorite meal was still sitting on the kitchen table.

A wave of anger shot through me as I threw the ground beef away and left the other items in the bag. I fixed me a bowl of cereal and called Mercedes. I was only able to get a few spoonfuls of cereal down because it simply hurt too much to chew. Mercedes was off every Wednesday so I knew she would be at home. During the time that we worked at Long John Silver's together we had developed a close relationship. I told her I needed a favor and gas money was involved. I explained in short detail what had transpired the day before and that I needed a ride home to my parent's house. I decided not to have mom and dad come get me since they had on two other occasions come and picked me up only for me to later return.

Mercedes agreed to take me home but stated it would be lunch time before she could come. I told her I'd be ready and waiting, I just hoped that Michael didn't come home for lunch to check in on me. While waiting on Mercedes, I packed my things and called home to let them know I was coming home.

I dreaded calling but I guess mom and dad expected it to happen sooner or later because she didn't seem surprised when I called. I didn't tell her all the details only that we had a fight. She was sympathetic and simply said we'll be here when you get here. Funny how the one place that I was so adamant about leaving, had become my safe haven.

Mercedes called just around 12:30pm to let me know she was on her way. Michael happened to call to check on me only moments after she called. Again, he sounded so concerned by asking how my jaw was feeling and if I were doing ok. He also kept apologizing about what he had done. The sad thing is I almost believed him. If only I could figure out how to reach that part of him that was so full of anger and turn off that switch, I'd have the perfect husband. But since I couldn't, I was returning home again with my head hung in shame.

Once I arrived home, my mom took one look at me and yelled, *"Oh my God! What did he do to you?"* I guess I did look pretty bad with a swollen jaw and lip. And the fact I was walking like an old lady. Mercedes and dad brought my bags in for me. I paid her some money for gas and thanked her for her help. After, telling me to take care of myself and promising to get my last check for me she left to return home.

After Mercedes left, dad told mom that she needed to take me to the doctor or emergency room to be checked out. He didn't ask me any questions; he just looked at me with eyes full of sadness and then walked into their bedroom. I don't know if he was sad that I had to experience such abuse or if he were sad because he felt I was a disgrace to the family. Whatever the reason, I knew I was the cause of the pain he was experiencing.
I didn't feel the need to go to the doctor. I advised mom I just needed to lie down. It wasn't like it was the first time that I had been in a fighting match with Michael and survived. So my argument was I'd be ok in a couple of days.

Dad heard the back and forth between mom and I and came out of the bedroom to back mom up. *"Now listen girl, either you go to the hospital or I'm going to call the law and tell them what happened for myself. Now do you want me to do that?"* He asked in a firm tone. He knew I didn't want to talk to the police or the law as he called them. So I obliged and agreed to go to the emergency room. Since it was the middle of the day, hopefully it wouldn't take forever and a day to be seen.

While mom was driving I concocted up a story to tell the nurses and doctors when they began questioning me about what happened. I didn't feel like talking so I closed my eyes and pretended to be sleepy. I just wanted to be lost in my own thoughts. I wondered what Michael was going to say once he came home and realized I was gone; or how long it was going to take for him to call with his lies and smooth talk to try to win me back.

We arrived at Troy Medical in a matter of ten minutes. Mom drove up to the Emergency entrance to let me out. I crept out of the car and mom came around to the passenger side to help me. A male nurse came through the sliding doors with a wheelchair as if they were waiting on me.

The nurse wheeled me to the registration desk all while asking me what had happened. The registration person began to ask me a series of personal questions: name, address, d.o.b, age, allergies, where does it hurt, etc. I answered each and every question just as methodically as she asked them.

Lastly, but not least the dreaded question was asked. *"And how did you get these injuries?"* She asked as she looked up from the form she was filling out. I was prepared to lie and say, I was in a car accident, but mom was standing right there so I just blurted out," *My husband and I got into a fight and No! I don't want to press charges."* As soon as I got the words out, I burst into tears. I was crying out of embarrassment and pain.

Mom immediately grabbed my hand and began to massage it in a loving manner as if to tell me it was ok. But she never said a word. The nurse that wheeled me in, ran over and knelt down beside me and rubbed my back and said, *"Not to worry, we'll take good care of you."* Though everyone was trying to be nice, I just wanted to crawl under a brick and hide.

After all the preliminary questions they put me in one of the little examining rooms and gave me a hospital gown to change into. Mom had to help me change out of my clothes. When she saw the many black and blue bruises all over my body she gasped in utter shock. *"Why you let that boy use you as a punching bag, Yolanda?"* She asked through a broken voice and eyes filled with tears. Seeing her cry caused the tears to stream down my face again. I managed to be the one to comfort her this time, and told her not to worry that I'd be ok. I don't know how convinced she was because I wasn't so sure myself. Only time would tell.

"Pregnant!!" Mom and I both exclaimed at the same time! Before I could have any x-rays done the nurse told me I had to have a pregnancy test done to make sure I was not pregnant. During the initial evaluation the nurse had asked about my last period. However, during the course of all that had went on in the last couple of months, I really hadn't kept up with my cycle.

After thinking about it, I realized the previous month my cycle was lighter than usual, and we were near the end of the month and Mother Nature hadn't shown up. After the pregnancy test came back as positive, the emergency room doctor did a physical exam and said I was approximately 10 ½ weeks pregnant.

I hadn't had any morning sickness. I had heard many complain about the nausea and vomiting but I had not experienced any of that. After careful thought I realized that some symptoms were there but I didn't relate it to pregnancy until at that moment. My breast had felt a little sore but I had attributed that to the fervent lovemaking sessions Michael and I had been having. I'd been craving a lot of spicy food lately. I was eating taco Supremes with extra hot sauce from Taco Bell almost every day; lastly, I was sleeping a lot but I thought I was just exhausted from work. I had not gained any noticeable weight. So when they said I was pregnant it really was a shock.

I came to the emergency room to ensure that my jaw or ribs were not broken but end up getting the shock of my life! Upon completion of the exam and x-rays, I had no broken bones but was just severely bruised up and pregnant!

How could this be happening to me at this time, I thought as we rode back home. Michael and I had tried everything under the sun to get pregnant in an effort to get mom and dad to allow us to get married; it didn't work. The only person that was getting pregnant was Tina. I had begun to think that I couldn't get pregnant. At the worse time in my life, my egg and his sperm decided to get acquainted with each other. I always heard that God had a sense of humor, only problem was that I wasn't laughing!

Truth of the matter was that I had mixed emotions. A part of me was kind of excited about being pregnant, while the other part of me was not. Being pregnant was going to be a new journey for me, a journey that I had not planned. It felt like I was reading a book. I knew the beginning and the ending but I didn't know anything about the middle. I was just told I was pregnant and I knew at the end of nine

months I would deliver a baby. However, I was clueless about what to expect during the pregnancy.
Seventeen years old, pregnant and separated from the baby's father. How awesome was that to share with everyone?

Mom had been very quiet on the ride back, I wasn't sure if that was a good thing or not. I couldn't tell if she was mad or happy about me contributing to the number of grand-children she already had. Up until that time I was the only child that did not have children.

I had only assumed that she was mad because all my life all I ever heard her say was *"Don't bring no baby in this house, if you do you will be on your own!* Mom would repeatedly exclaim this mostly anytime I were going out on a date! If she had only known that her worries weren't just with my dates but with her husband. Now that I reflect on the many times that Dad invaded my innocence, it's amazing that I didn't get pregnant. He didn't seem to worry about it either, because he never used protection and he knew I was not on birth control. All that was irrelevant now, I had bigger problems to deal with.

Daddy was sitting in the kitchen waiting on us when we got back home. His face was not what I wanted to see at the moment. I hadn't prepared myself mentally to listen to his ranting and raving about bringing a reproach on the family; how he had an image to uphold as a Pastor and man of God; and how I never listened to anything they told me. I just did not want to be preached too, but there he were waiting and looking like he had a word for the congregation as I walked into the kitchen with mom close behind me.

"Well how far along are you?" He knowingly asked as I walked towards the hallway that led to my room. I stopped dead in my tracks and turned around to face him. He didn't go to the hospital with us; mom hadn't had time to call him. Therefore, how did he know? I thought as I walked back towards him. I asked him how he knew I was pregnant being that I had just found out. He claimed he had seen it in a dream. Dad went on to say that is why he was so adamant about me going to the doctor; he knew I was pregnant.

Wow! Was all I could say. You would just have to know the other side of my dad to understand what I was thinking. My dad was always having dreams, visions and premonitions about things. Most times mom and I would not pay him any attention when he claimed he saw things or had a dream. However, there were those times when we experienced the realism of his dreams. I guess in this instance his dream became my reality.

I grabbed a glass of water and took a Hydrocodone pill for pain and went to lay down. I was in a lot of pain both physically and emotionally. I just wanted to float away on a cloud but since that couldn't happen, I would accept a deep sleep. I was wishing that I wake up and all of this be a dream! It wasn't.

Months later I was in a hospital bed in Montgomery, Alabama waiting for my baby to come. I was nervous, scared and anxious since the doctor told me that my baby wouldn't live. My water broke one night while Michael and I were lying in the bed watching TV. Ironically, it happened two days after we got into an argument and he pushed me and my stomach hit a brick wall. Of course, I didn't tell anyone that bit of information.

Michael claimed he didn't mean to push me and that he was playing as he grabbed the bag of chips from my hand. When I proved to be just a little bit quicker and snatched the chips back he pushed me. You decide. In my reality Michael was never too happy that I was pregnant. Oh yes he said he was and initially when I told him I was pregnant he was enthused. However, after I agreed to move back and be a family his enthusiasm seemed to fade.

I made the decision to return home because I was pregnant and felt that maybe the baby was the missing piece to our happiness. In addition, I didn't want my parents to have to be responsible for me and my child. Even though I was married, I still felt funny with being pregnant and at home with my parents. I guess mom's command; *"Don't bring any babies in this house"* were forever etched in my brain!

Michael rushed me to the hospital in Brundidge after I felt a trickle of water run down my leg. For a slight moment I thought I was peeing on myself. I jumped up and ran to the bathroom as soon as I made it to the bathroom water just gushed everywhere! I screamed for Michael because this couldn't be happening. I was only 6 ½ months pregnant! When Michael saw that my water had broke he transformed into the loving, doting husband. I could tell he was nervous too but yet he became very attentive. He helped me change clothes and got me in the car. He called his family and let them know we were headed to the hospital. Once arriving at the hospital the nursed quickly put me in a room and hooked up the baby monitor.

The doctor came in to check to make sure that my water had indeed broke and to see if my cervix had dilated. I definitely didn't like this doctor that was on call. He didn't have an ounce of sympathy. He was very dismal in his statements. *"Mrs. Houston, you are only 6 ½ months pregnant and most babies have a difficult time living at this stage of the pregnancy. You are not even in the last trimester yet. Therefore, I have to tell you that your baby more than likely will die."*

I will never ever forget those words. I burst into tears and Michael just held me and let me cry. I couldn't even gauge Michael's level of disappointment because I was so engulfed in my own anxiety. Being that Brundidge was a small town hospital they decided to send me to Montgomery, Alabama to the hospital that had a Neonatal unit. Though the doctor didn't think that the baby would live he sent me there because that hospital was more equipped to care for premature births.

I remember very little about the ambulance ride to Montgomery. I just know that Michael said he would drive down. For insurance purposes they would not allow him to ride with me. Baptist Medical had to be the biggest and busiest hospital I had ever seen. There were people lying on carts in the hallways, doctors, nurses, and medical staff running all over the place. I was totally overwhelmed.

I was checked in and placed in a semi-private room with another pregnant lady that wouldn't stop talking. I think she was trying to be nice but I didn't want to talk. I wanted my mother, but sadly enough she was unable to be there. Dad told me that mom had to fly to Michigan to check on my grandmother who was really sick. Therefore, I was alone with no family or friends until Michael got there.

Two days later, around 4 O'clock in the morning, I was awaken with sharp pains in my stomach. The pain continued and intensified rather quickly. Up until this time, I had been on complete bed rest and had not had any contractions. The pain became so intense that I woke up my roommate with my moaning and groaning. She was used to being pregnant because this was her third pregnancy, therefore, she knew what to expect. *"Sounds like somebody in labor, you better call the nurse, she says groggily."*

I hit the call button for the nurse and told her that I was in pain. Sure enough I was in labor. The contractions were coming five minutes apart. I had never in my life felt such pain. Those pains were worse than menstrual cramps and I didn't think anything could be worse than that.

The nurse called Michael for me to let him know I was in labor. He happened to have an Aunt that lived in Montgomery so he was at her house. I was taken to Labor

& Delivery where I was monitored regularly on my progress. Again I was placed in a semi private room with another patient. This patient was not talking she was hollering and screaming at the top of her lungs as if someone was killing her. Though my pains were bad, they had not reached the point where I was screaming. But her loudness added to my fear and I prayed that I would not be in as much pain as she were.

Michael finally made it to the hospital and they let him in to see me only for a few moments. He was not allowed to stay in the room with me. We were told that once I go into the actual delivery room he would be able to be with me. I was so upset and began to cry because I was scared and needed him to be with me the whole time. Here I am scared to death, worried that my baby will die; without my mother and in a strange place and my husband can't be there to console me. I was at such an unexplainable place and I didn't like it.

However, the good thing was that periodically they would allow Michael to come and talk with me for about five minutes. He seemed so concerned and upset that he couldn't be there either. But knowing he was there in the hospital was comforting.

Prior to going into labor I had agreed to have *'twilight anesthesia'* Epidurals weren't as popular as they are now. A friend of mine told me not to have an epidural because if it was administered wrong I would be paralyzed. I definitely didn't want to be paralyzed so I went with the twilight. Well the twilight ended up being *a twi-lie!!!* It didn't help with my pain. All it did was make me groggy I would doze off to sleep and wake up in more pain.

By the eighth hour of being in labor I was screaming like my neighbor and begging to be put to sleep or something, anything, just get this baby out of me!!! I guess the nurse that was attending to our room was tired of the entire ruckus we were doing.

She was an older looking black lady with grey hair. A little on the short side and slightly plumb; her face was very stern. She boldly entered the room and went straight to the lady on the other side of the green curtain that separated our beds. *"Listen here, I'm only going to say this once so listen good. You were not doing all that hollering when you were getting this baby so you don't need to be hollering now that it's coming. So lie in this bed and calm your nerves, everybody in this hospital know you in here. All that hollering is not going to make either of your babies come any faster! Do you hear me, she firmly said."*

Though she was on the other side of the curtain talking to the other patient I knew she was talking to me too. The lady tried to plead her case and say how much pain she was in, but Ms. Nurselady was not hearing it. *"Well! You should have learned your lesson the first time but you didn't because you back up in here again, she sternly stated."* I didn't think it was right for the nurse to talk to her like she did but what could either of us do, other than lay there and listen to her scold us. When Ms. Nurselady came from behind that curtain and looked at me as if to say, *'the same thing applies to you!'* I just held my breath during the contraction and looked back at her until she left the room. I didn't want to be scolded too.

I tried to obey and not scream and holler but the pain had become too intense. If I could have reached inside myself and pulled the baby out I would have. I thought this child was never going to come out. The clock was directly in front of me on the wall. I kept watching the clock and around the 13th hour I was deliriously frantic! And just when I thought I was going to pass out from the pain; I felt something pop between my legs. I could feel something but I was scared to move. I didn't even push the nurse button. I just was yelling, *"Nurse! Nurse! Help Nurse!!"* The same little stern nurse came flying into the room. *"Chile! What is wrong with you? And why are you doing all this hollering?"*

I told her that I felt something between my legs. And I explained what happened. She quickly put on her gloves and went under the sheets to take a look. She told me to spread my legs and bend my knees. As soon as I did she yelped, *"Chile you delivering this baby on your own! Be still and don't push!"* She ran out the room and within seconds came back with another nurse. They were talking between themselves how the doctor would not have time to get there. It seems my baby's head was already out. She reached under the covers and told me to push one good time. I pushed and she pulled this seemingly lifeless baby out.

At approximately 5:15p.m on October 19, 1987. I became a mother! Everything after that was a blur. I remember a room full of people coming into the room and I heard her say, *"It's a girl."* The next thing I remember was waking up in another room and Michael was holding my hand. I immediately asked where my baby was at. And he told me that she was taken to a special nursery unit.

Apparently, I had a panic attack after Mynesha was delivered. The doctor gave me something in my IV to relax me. I don't remember any of that. But I guess from the stress of the delivery and thinking that the baby was going to die, I panicked. The nurse soon came in to check on me and give me an update on the baby. She told me that Mynesha weighed only 2lbs and was having problems breathing because her lungs were not fully developed.

She assured me that they were doing everything to make sure my baby lived and once I was strong enough they would let me see her. Somehow I had developed a bladder infection and they were giving me antibiotics to get the fever down and to treat the bladder infection. My nurse says, I developed the infection because my womb was open for a few days before I actually had the baby. I really didn't care about all of that; I just wanted to see my baby. I was still feeling anxious but I was also still very tired and sleepy.

Michael wasn't saying very much he just told me to get some rest and that he would be back in the morning. I think as soon as he left I went to sleep. Sleep had become my best friend because when I was sleep I had no worries; no pain and no fears. Sleep came easy but waking up was hard.

When I finally laid eyes on Mynesha I was overwhelmed with many emotions; joy, sadness, fear and hope. Joy because Michael and I finally had a child together; his first daughter. I felt sadness; because our child had to fight for her life in a plastic incubator with several tubes running through her body. Fear gripped me, because I didn't know if she would make it. My mind was still reeling from what the doctor in Brundidge told me. However, because I had been raised in church all my life and had constantly heard the word preached. I was still hopeful, hopeful because I yet believed in God and if I didn't know anything else I knew how to pray.

I stayed in the hospital four days before I was ready to be released. Sadly, I had to leave Mynesha in the hospital. Surprisingly, my baby girl was a fighter she was yet holding on. I knew when the nurse told me that Mynesha had accidently pulled the breathing tube out of her mouth and was breathing on her own; I had a fighter and she was going to make it. Though that was a sign of progress she still had a long way to go. I wouldn't be able to take my baby home until she was at least five pounds and her lungs were more developed. I was happy to be leaving the hospital but sad to be leaving without my baby.

Throughout this whole ordeal Michael hadn't shown much emotion especially after Mynesha was born. He didn't say much about the baby he was more concerned with when we would be going home. I understood that because I too had had enough of the hospital and was ready to go home. But I felt empty without my baby. I entered into the hospital with a baby attached within me; with little hope that she would live one complete day.

But I was leaving without her, unattached and empty handed. Surreal as it was, it was reality; my baby girl was being left behind. As I was wheeled to the front door of the hospital tears lined my face. For the first time in my life, I was experiencing what it meant to be a mother. Funny how your life can change in a moment, a minute, or a day, mine had.

Michael waited for me in the car, the nurse helped me in and handed me a small gift bag full of parenting information and samples of baby products. I was told to call anytime to check on Mynesha and that I could visit whenever I wanted too. I couldn't wait to come back to visit.

As soon as I was in the car Michael sped off like he was running from the police! I looked at him like he was crazy as I struggled to put my seat belt on. I didn't say anything because he kept looking straight ahead as if he didn't see me looking at him. I could tell something was on his mind I figured he was feeling stressed about leaving our baby behind too. I would soon realize that was far from the truth.

The first two weeks after being at home were a living hell for more than one reason. I was missing my baby terribly! My breast were full of milk and silly me thought that if I tried to squeeze it out that it would alleviate the weightiness of them. Little did I know that when you squeeze the milk out it is telling your body to replace more; plus me squeezing made them more sensitive. I was a miserable camper.

Michael wasn't giving me any emotional support. He treated me like a plague especially since we couldn't have sex. After work he would stay out late somewhere, I could only imagine where. Mentally, I was stressed because Michael dropped a bombshell on me as we traveled home from the hospital. I replayed his words over and over liked a scratched record in my head. *"Whose baby is that because I don't believe it's mine?"* He said in a matter of fact kind of way."

I thought my eyes were going to pop out of my head from the shock. I was stunned, surprised and caught off guard from his question! How dare he question if Mynesha was his. Who else did he think it could be? While I was in the middle of giving him a piece of my mind, *"You have the nerve to ask me such a stupid question! When you are............When you Are........the father! "*

My statements started out strong and powerful but in midstream I had to change my intended words. I intended to say, *"You have the nerve to ask me such a stupid question! When you are the only person I've been with!"* Before I could form those words, the truth showed up in my mind. Truth was Michael was not the only person I had been with. There was one other person, Princeton! Therefore, I had to think quickly and maintain the passion in my words, *"You Are the Father"* was all I could muster up, but I said it as confident as I could. Praying and hoping that I was convincing. And just think Maury Povich is now getting credit for my statements

Michael's only defense was that Mynesha didn't look like him! Well Mynesha didn't look like anybody because she was so tiny and with all the tubes she was attached too you could barely see her tiny body. We went back and forth half the ride home that day about Michael's paternity. When he threw up in my face that he didn't know what I was doing while we were separated. I came back violently and screamed *"But we know what you were doing! Who you been doing! And what you probably still doing now! Don't we?"*

I guess I made my point clear because he shut up about it. I didn't deny his accusations but I sure wasn't going to admit to anything either. I merely turned the tables on him and stated the facts about his indiscretions; He had no proof of mine but he had two crumb snatchers to validate my case and plus I had seen it with my own eyes. I guess that old cliché' is true, *'Don't throw stones if you live in glass houses.'*

Anyway! Regardless of what might slightly be true, deep down in my heart I knew Michael was Mynesha's father. I just hope my heart was not lying to me. Therefore you can see how frenzied my life had been since becoming a mother. However, even with the chaos it seemed I had grown up overnight. Something within me was different. So much so, I decided to leave Michael for good!

I finally realized that I was tired of the drama filled life I was living. I thought once upon a time that a baby would transform our lives but it hasn't. It actually seemed to push us farther apart, maybe because Mynesha was sickly and premature and we hadn't had time to fully bond with her. But whatever the case I was tired of the *'what if's'*, I had to deal with the, *'what is'* of my life. The *'what if's'* of life are fiction but the *'what is'* of life are factual.

I had called mom and dad to ask them to come and get me while Michael was at work the next day. As usual they were there for me without many questions asked. I made the decision to leave the night after Michael and I had this big blow out about the passion mark I saw on his neck. I happened to walk into the bathroom while he was getting out the shower and saw it.

Red marks show up well on a fair complexion man. When I asked him about it he immediately went into defense mode and tried to lie about it by saying he got bit by some bug and that I was just paranoid. But I was not buying the bull crap he was trying to sell me. I had been down this road far too many times so I recognized the lie straight from the beginning. We went a round or two with arguing about everything and nothing! I was fed up and I really didn't have time to worry about what he was doing. I was worried about my baby.

Mom and dad arrived about nine o'clock the next morning as planned. I was in my bedroom packing the last bit of my clothes while mom was in the living room watching TV. All of a sudden I heard the front door open and I thought it was dad coming from outside until I heard Michael's voice as he spoke to mom. I already knew it was about to be some drama when he saw me packing my things.

We lived in a small one bedroom house. The bedroom was separated from the living room by one wall. I could walk out of my bedroom right into the kitchen and off from the kitchen was the bathroom. The kitchen did have a back door. I give this description to prepare you for what happened next.

Michael enters into the bedroom seemingly calm and grabs me and gives me a hug. As he is holding me he is whispering, *"Don't leave me, Yolanda don't leave me"* As I'm trying to pull away from him and tell him to let me go his grip gets tighter. He is still whispering in my ear but the words are getting intense, I could feel his emotions changing from calmness to anger.

Since I was trying to pull away from him he swiftly and in one move shifts us to the bed and he has me pinned to the bed with his body. I'm steady trying to get him to let me go without alarming my mother who is clueless as to what is happening. Once I realize he is not going to let me go, I yell for my mom to make him get off me. Her reasoning with him from the other room was not working. Mind you she can't see what is going on because of how the bed was positioned in the bedroom.

Mom was a plump lady and had arthritis badly in one leg so she couldn't move very fast. So mom screams for my dad because she could hear the intensity in the room. Michael turned into a mad man when he heard mom calling for dad who was outside piddling around on his car.

He picked me up and drug me across the bed; for a split second I was in plain view of my mother's eyes. It all happened so fast she couldn't do anything but scream! This joker proceeds to drag me over the glass kitchen table that was beautifully set up with cheap china plates and crystal glasses bought from Roses department store.

I could hear the glasses and plates crashing to the floor along with my mom's screams as we hit the back door. As he yanked me down the cement steps, my back felt like it hit all four of them. He has my hands over my head and he is dragging me like I'm a toy wagon. If I had not experienced it myself I would think it was from a movie scene. I'm screaming, *"Stop, Help!"* and trying to get a loose.

When I started screaming he jerked my arms so hard I thought he had pulled them out of socket. He firming told me to shut up or he would kill me as he is pulling me over a small wire fence that separated our back yard to an adjoining street. I am in so much pain and scared for my life. I really thought I was going to die. I literally saw my Eighteen years of life flash before my eyes.

It is strange how sometimes you pray to die but when you are faced with death you pray to live. I was silently praying to live. I had to live for Mynesha, if my life meant nothing hers did. Once we made if over the fence he made me stand up and when I did he put a box cutter to my back and told me to walk. I obeyed like a helpless victim. I was a victim at the hands of my own husband. We walked a couple of blocks to a nearby apartment complex.

It's funny how we passed many houses and several cars passed us by and no one, not one soul noticed anything strange. My hair was all disheveled, clothes dirty and tattered and this guy is walking closely upon me as if we were Siamese twins; and nobody saw anything? I'll never forget wishing somebody would drive by or walk by and say something. No one ever did. When we made it to the back of the apartment complex, I didn't know what he was going to do. He was out of breath and I just knew I was one moment away from dying.

My mom and dad had no clue as to where I was, no one was around to call the police and I was too tired, hurt and scared to try to run. Michael was still holding the box cutter to my back and rambling on about something, I don't remember what. I was too busy thinking how all this was going to pan out. I looked up and strangely enough saw the man I couldn't have been happier to see; my Dad!!

He came around the corner of that apartment dressed in black dress pants a grey long-sleeved shirt and a black tie with a crowbar in his hands! Talking about saving the day! Once my Horror but now my Hero! *"Michael, I don't want no mess out of you, let her go and yall come on and get in this car!, he angrily stated!"* Without hesitation Michael complied. He released his grip on me and we followed dad to the car.

Now the standing applause goes to my mom. When we got in the back seat of that car my mom was raging mad! I had never seen her in such an uproar! She turned around in that seat and faced Michael with a Coke bottle raised in her hand, *"Boy! Are you crazy or you done lost your mind? This girl just got out the hospital; don't you know her body ain't healed yet? You could have killed her! I got a notion to throw this here bottle upside your head! Don't you ever put your hands on her again, if you do, I won't think twice about what I'm going to do to you!! Do you hear me talking to you?"* She said all in one breath! Michael kept his eyes on her but humbly answered, *"Yes maam"* My dad tried to get her to calm down but she was too upset to calm down.

I didn't say a word because I was in awe of her reaction. In all my days of living I had never seen that side of my mom. She was normally a sweet, humble and soft spoken person. That day proved otherwise, mom had another side and the devil himself had brought it out of her. Praise be to the devil one time because I was happy to know that she would fight for her child. I knew at that very moment that this woman loved me!

We made it back to the house and Michael got out our car and got in his and left. Dad went in the house with me to get the rest of my stuff. We packed the car and left. When we got in the car I asked dad how he found us. He simply said, *"The Lord showed him."* My mom confirmed it because she said they drove around a few streets and he suddenly said, I know where they are and came right to where we were. I know it had to be God because where we were was not visible to the street. We were behind the apartment complex. Once we crossed that fence we could have went in any direction.

I was happy that he found us but confusion quickly set in. Why would God talk to my dad in spite of all the bad things he did to me? If he did talk to him, Did my dad listen all the time? My dad used to always say that God sent me to him; could that possibly be true since he allowed him to find me. Can you understand why my mind is filled with confusion? What kind of God would allow an innocent child to be abused by the only father she knows? Then this same man shows her compassion time after time in her times of trouble. And God uses this same man to rescue her from a close call of death. What kind of God is this? I have questions that I may never have the answer too, but at that moment even in the midst of my confusion, I was glad to still be alive.

Life without Michael was better but not perfect. I had finally accepted the fact that Michael and I could not and would not be together. I had more important things to think about other than Michael. Mynesha was my main focus. Mynesha was three months old before she was allowed to come home and she only weighed five pounds by that time. I was grateful that mom was there to help me because I never would have been able to take care of her. She was sickly and in and out the hospital the first year of her life. Her immune system was weak and she was easy to catch colds which lead to pneumonia. Of course Michael acted like we didn't exist most of the time. He ended up dating a girl I used to go to school with. I didn't care because while she thought she was getting a treat; I knew she was getting a trick.

I have to admit that I messed around with him a couple of times after the fact but it were on my terms and not his. He had lost his control over me and I never went back to him. In fact I filed for divorce through legal aid and was granted a divorce in about ninety days. From the time I married Michael to the time our divorce was final totaled about 2 1/2 yrs. It seemed those were the longest years of my life, they definitely were the worst years of my life; with the exception of Mynesha being born. Michael threatened me when I first filed for divorce that he was going to put a hit out on me. I was fearful for a moment because I had experienced his wrath, but I soon pushed pass that fear and handled my business. Something within me was determined to live a life free of fear, of course he never made good on his word.

The small possibility about Princeton being Mynesha's daddy was soon put to rest. After all the tubes were taken off her and she had time to develop into her own, it was obvious who her daddy was. She had Michael's hazel eyes, and even if she didn't have his eyes, everything else about her wreaked of Michael. She looked as if Michael had spit her out himself and she continues to look more like him than any of his children.

It was funny because until I brought her home even Princeton thought she might be his. He asked me one day when I was over there visiting if Mynesha was his. At that moment I couldn't give him a definite answer. I merely told him that it's a slight possibility since there were at least two occasions that Princeton and I did not use protection. He was worried about what his parents would say if he had a baby, but he also seemed to welcome the idea of possibly being a father. When I told him he was not the father he showed both relief and sadness.

Though Princeton would have made the better father, I didn't want him to have to alter his life because of a baby. He had too much going for him; College scholarships and possibly pro ball. I was happy to have him as my friend. Many things had changed with Princeton and I. We still carried on our little rendezvous from time to time but we both had started seeing other people.

Shortly after my divorce was final I got involved with a considerably older man. It was unexpected. I met him while hanging out with some friends. Things between us quickly progressed. Even though I had been married and divorced; I was still marriage minded. I thought that was the way of life at least that is what I had been taught. Jacoby and I moved in together after he found out I was pregnant and we even talked of getting married. Talk about being happy! He was very pleased that I was pregnant because he didn't have any children. I didn't want for anything while I was pregnant. Mynesha was only a year old when I found out I was pregnant. Mom and dad agreed to take care of Mynesha for me after finding out I was pregnant again. They knew I was not prepared to take care of her and another baby; and I couldn't deny that fact. They were also helping to pay for her medical expenses, not to mention they were very attached to Mynesha. It was hard to leave my baby when I moved in with Jacoby but I was over at their house a lot spending time with her.

Those same parents that drilled me not to bring a baby home were now lovingly and willingly taking care of my child. I was more than appreciative for their kindness. Dad still acted like a father and as if nothing had ever happened between us. I had started to loosen up and forget what he had done when one day he said something to me that made me cringe. I went over to ride to church with dad one night because he had to preach at a little church in a nearby town. He asked me to go and sing for him. Mom didn't go because it was in the dead of winter and she didn't want to take Mynesha out in the cold.

Things were going fine until he started this crazy conversation," *You know I used to always like being with my first wife when she was pregnant. That's the best sex that a man can ever have*", he said while looking over at me while he drove. Suddenly I became fearful as I remembered all the things he used to do to me as a child. I became frightened because we were on a lonely country road traveling to church; I wasn't sure if he had plans to pull over somewhere and attempt to rape me before we got to church. I guess the look on my face let him know that I wasn't interested because he then said, *"I guess you wouldn't be interested in anything like that, would you"* I was speechless, I just shook my head and mumbled No.

He didn't say anything else and continued driving to the church. That night I sang my usual requested song, *'Precious Lord'*. I really needed him to take my hand and help me stand because I was weak and worn. Not only did I sing from the bottom of my heart, dad preached the house down. They were shouting and praising God as if Jesus himself had walked in the room. Again, I was a mass of confusion. How could he preach with such power and anointing when he had just tried to seduce me? I didn't understand this God that I had been taught about all my life. I believed he was real but I sure didn't understand his ways.

Soon after Jamiria was born I got a job and moved out on my own. My relationship with Jacoby was short lived he was kind and generous and we had some good times together but he loved the bottle more than he cared about me. I couldn't take anymore of Jacoby's alcoholic ways. I tried but you have to understand that I wasn't raised around people who drink; I didn't even drink. Yes, life was better with Jacoby than it was with Michael but I still wasn't completely happy. I raised my concerns to him about drinking so much but it went in one ear and out the other.

My nagging only caused him to try and hide the alcohol and how much he was drinking. He would come home late at night reeking of alcohol and then want to kiss and sex me up. I wanted to throw up! I would give into him because I wanted to prevent a verbal argument and keep him from waking up Jamiria. When he was in a drunken state and didn't get his way he would get all loud and boisterous. His ranting and raving would wake the baby and then I'd have double trouble.

Oftentimes, I felt like Celie from the Color Purple. I would just lay there and let him do his business. It would only take him a few minutes whenever he was drunk. Sometimes, I would let my mind travel far away while he was on me doing his thing. Other times I would lie there and cry in silence and pray he would hurry up. I had learned as a child how to let my mind release me from the things I didn't want or know how to cope with. I did it with Dad and Michael and I used it frequently with

Jacoby. By doing so, things didn't seem so bad; my body was in one place but my mind was in another. I guess you call that coping skills.

Living on my own was stressful; I could barely make ends meet. This was the first time that I lived on my own. Life was hard. I didn't have a regular baby sitter so often times I missed work unless my senior citizen neighbor agreed to keep Jamiria for me. I quickly fell behind on my rent so I was dodging the landlord. Mom and Dad had moved back to Lafayette, GA and had taken Mynesha with them.

Dad tried to get me to move back with them but I refused. I didn't like Lafayette and plus I didn't want to be under his watchful eye or to give him opportunity to make a move on me. He made a great plea by offering to get me my own place and help me get a car but I knew I would have to pay him back in ways that I wasn't willing to do. I would miss Mynesha dearly but I took my chances and tried to make it on my own.

I gave it my best shot but I ended up getting fired because I had missed too many days from work. I applied and was approved for welfare but the check did not cover all my expenses. I tried to hold it together and at least keep my rent up but I was still behind. By the time I paid $200 rent out of the $358 monthly welfare check, it left little money to pay utilities and food. Jacoby was my fall back person, he was very good about helping me with Jamiria whenever I called and asked him for something. However, that meant having to give him sex. Yep, it sounds like I was a low class prostitute; call it what you want but I call it survival; I was doing what I had to do to take care of my child.

I think it sad that a man would ask for restitution in order to help take care of the child that he asked for. However, it is what it is and I did what I did; bottom line. At least I was not out on the street sexing strangers. Since I was going to have sex I may as well have it with my child's father. It was worth it, especially if it meant my baby having diapers and food to eat. I eventually had Jacoby placed on child support but because I was getting a welfare check the State kept that money to pay back the money I was receiving from them. It was a win lose situation.

Since I wasn't working I decided to visit my sister Darissa and her daughter Karla. I caught a ride with an old high school friend, Antonio. The game plan was that he was to pick me back up on his way back home that Sunday night. Well when we arrived to Brundidge Darissa was still at work so I went to my friend's house with him until she got home. I had known Antonio for a long time. We went to school together and our families knew each other. Therefore, I felt safe.

Little did I know that he was going to try and get me to have sex with him.

He fed me this lame game that he had always been attractive to me but never said anything because he knew I was involved with someone. I already knew where he was going with this so I cut him off quickly. I told him I was not interested because I was still seeing somebody. That was a lie, but I had to tell him something to get him to stop coming on to me. Plus I was not attracted to his sloppy looking self. Well it seemed to work and he later took me back over Darissa's house and he said he would see me on Sunday. You already know what happened next; he never showed up.

I kept calling his home number and no one answered. Darissa didn't have a car so she couldn't take me back. I couldn't think of any one that could take me back home. I was stranded. Darissa finally thought of someone that may take me home. It was the brother of one of her girlfriends. She told me that Ryan was a cool guy and that she knew he would probably take me back home to Troy.

Darissa was cool with Ryan's family because she often hung out with his sister Jennifer. She got me the phone number from Jennifer so that I could call and speak to Ryan. I was scared to call him because I didn't know this guy but Darissa assured me that Jennifer had already given him a heads up about me calling. I didn't have any other options so I called Ryan Monday evening when I thought he would be home from work.

As I dialed the numbers I was trying to think what I would say when he answered. Here I am calling a total stranger to ask him would he take me home. The last time I hopped in the car of a total stranger I got raped so anyone should understand my apprehension. However, the difference this time is that the reference came from my sister and I trusted her.

When Ryan answered the phone, we went through the typical greeting and introduction. I explained my situation and how I got stranded. Ryan laughed and joked that I should have given the guy what he wanted because it's our job to help the needy. We both laughed as I stated, *"Well I hope that you will help the needy and take me home!"* Surprisingly, Ryan was very easy to talk too and he made me laugh; we had an instant connection and many things in common. We both had been married and divorced. He had a two year old son that lived in another city and of course I had a six month old daughter. He understood the experience of being married and divorced. He seemed to have solid family background and a great upbringing. Just talking to him put me at ease about him driving me home.

Our conversation was good that he actually asked me out on a date. We agreed to go to a movie before we rode to Troy. How ironic is that? I call just trying to get a ride home and end up with a date. When I told Darissa she was overly excited, if I didn't know any better I would think that she had set this whole thing up. In any case I was glad that she thought of Ryan to take me home.

Darissa took me shopping at one of the little clothing stores in Brundidge to buy an inexpensive outfit. I hadn't planned on going on a date so I had only brought a pair of jeans and a couple of different shirts to get me through the weekend. I felt that I could have worn the jeans and shirt I brought but Darissa was against it. She said, Ryan was a real man and first impressions were a lasting impression. Therefore, she thought I should make a lasting impression with a new outfit. Cato's clothing store happened to have a sale and we found a cute pair of teal blue denim jeans with a checkered teal blue and white shirt. I wore white tennis shoes with silver earrings. I was cute if I had to say so myself but I always thought I were cute.

Ryan picked me up from Darissa's house. When I met him in the living room, I wasn't immediately smitten, I didn't get butterflies or anything like that. I actually was quite calm. Everything was easy and familiar as if we had known each other a long time. Ryan spoke and gave me a hug. I instantly noticed his muscular arms as he hugged me tight. The cologne he wore was sweet to my nostrils. He was dressed nicely in some Levi Jeans and a red short sleeve T-shirt. He stood about 5'9 medium muscular build. A thin neatly trimmed mustached lined his thick upper lip. Overall he was a nice looking but average type guy.

The date with Ryan went nicely. I don't remember the movie that we saw because we talked and laughed through most of it. After the movie we headed to Troy. I really didn't want the evening to end because I was enjoying myself so much. He seemed to be enjoying himself also. I don't know who laughed the most him or me.

Once we arrived in Troy, I directed him how to get to my little apartment. When he pulled in my drive way I noticed a red sign on my door but couldn't make out the writing. As I approached the door I was able to make out the letters before I reached my porch. EVICTED! Guess how surprised and embarrassed I was as I read the words.

I quickly snatched the sign as I unlocked the door. Ryan asked me was everything ok? I lied and told him yeah, *"I have the rent money but I just didn't make it back here in time to pay. The Land lord is very strict, but I'll pay tomorrow. I lied."* I guess I was convincing because he didn't keep probing. We sat and talked for a moment but he didn't stay long because he had work the next day. At that point, it was a good thing because my happy high had become a depressing downer.

To make a long story short, Ryan and I dated briefly and later got married. Well to tell the truth we really didn't date. He came back to Troy the following weekend and we went out to eat and then to a club. Ryan was so caring and easy to talk too; I ended up telling him that I really was being evicted. I had managed to buy some time, because I gave the landlord part of the money.

I had no clue where I was going to live. Ryan still lived at home with his parents; therefore moving in with him was not an option. Surprisingly, Ryan's brother had moved in with his girlfriend and was looking for someone to rent his house. Problem solved, Ryan and I moved in his brother's house and life was good, or so I thought!

More Mess

As you can tell my life has been full of heartache, misery and sadness. So when Ryan came into my life I thought finally life was going to be great. Well there is not always light at the end of the tunnel; at least not for me. More misery and mess was at the end of mine.
About a month after moving in with Ryan I found out I was pregnant and of course the baby was not his. I hid it from him for as long as I could because I was afraid to tell him. I knew he was going to flip. He was such a good father to Jamiria but what man was going to stay with a woman that is pregnant with another man's child. Can you imagine the guilt and emotional stress I was experiencing?

My secret wouldn't remain a secret for long because Ryan had begun to notice the difference in my body. Plus once during an intimate moment he said he tasted milk; need I say more? I thought the cat was out the bag at that moment but I gave him a lame excuse, *"maybe all my milk hasn't dried up from Jamiria."* He accepted the excuse and carried on. However, I knew I had to do something and fast.

All my life I have had to lie and cover up the truth in order to protect myself. I was thinking of every lie that I could tell to prevent Ryan from finding out the truth. I thought about an abortion, but I was too scared to follow through, plus I didn't have any money. My only option was to tell the truth and let the pieces fall where they lie.

I had made up in my mind that I would just pack up and move back to Lafayette where mom and dad were until I could get on my feet. I knew they wouldn't be happy about me being pregnant but Dad would help me get my own place, plus I'd be there to help with Mynesha.

I told Ryan one night that I thought I was pregnant and needed to go to the doctor. What I didn't tell him was that I knew it wasn't his. He immediately asked me was it his and I told him I was not sure. Half-truths. I went to the doctor as scheduled and the doctor confirmed that I was about three months pregnant. When I told Ryan that the baby wasn't his, I could see the hurt on his face. I was crying crocodile tears; I had hurt the man that I cared about and the one man that seemingly loved me for me. I told him that I didn't know that I was pregnant when we got together. Truth. He asked who the father was and I told him it was an ex, and that I didn't have any further contact with him and I didn't want him to know. Again, that was part of the truth.

Princeton and I hadn't seen each other since the last time we were together; three months ago. It was one of those, *'for old times' sake,'* moments. Princeton had just signed to play college football in Tennessee. We hooked up to say goodbye, little did I know that our goodbye would result in a baby. It wasn't planned but our chemistry and reminiscing led us back to a familiar and enjoyable place; in each other's arms.

The truth was that I didn't want Princeton to know because it would have totally changed his life and ruined his chances of a football career. Princeton had just been signed to play college ball and I was not going to take that away from him. To this day, he never knew I was pregnant with his child.

To my amazement, Ryan said well I will be the father! I thought I would faint from shock. I couldn't believe my ears. I asked him was he sure and he said yes. *"I can't blame you for something that happened before we got together, it's not like you cheated on me, plus I love you," he said while wiping tears from my eyes.* At that moment, I thought Ryan was my angel sent from heaven. Twice he had come to my rescue.

I never expected the reaction I received from him. I was worried about what his family would think but he told me it didn't matter; it was his decision. Word spread like wild fire that I was pregnant with another man's baby. We had to deal with the negative comments of a few people but most people didn't seem to care. When Ryan's family learned that the baby wasn't his they didn't treat me any different and continued to treat me as part of the family.

Did I mention that Ryan's dad was a Baptist preacher and constantly preached to us that we needed to get married? He didn't believe in shacking. No matter how I tried I couldn't get away from the word of God; I couldn't hide from the truth and what I knew to be right. Although, I knew marriage was a good thing, I wasn't quite sure if I was ready to get married again. I had been through one bad marriage and none of my relationships afterwards were successful. However, the pressure was on us to get married. Ryan's brother had even gotten married. We both had started attending church with Ryan's parents and every time we went to church it seemed that the preacher were talking too us. We eventually decided to get married and we did so on my twentieth birthday, November 11, 1989. Ryan's father actually married us in our living room. I wasn't excited about getting married but I knew it was the right thing to do. I can't even say that I was in-love with Ryan but I did love him. I'm not even sure if Ryan was in-love either but I do know he loved me too. I would soon learn just how much he loved me.

Everybody knew how protective Ryan was of me. He didn't want me to go anywhere without him. He had to know my every move at all times. He said it was because he wanted to make sure I was safe. I once made the mistake of telling him that a mutual friend had given me a compliment and he went ballistic! He claimed that the guy was trying to come on to me. *"Ryan that is crazy, I'm six months pregnant, what would he want me for,"* I screamed back at him. After many conversations like this, I came to understand that Ryan was just a little jealous. I thought it was cute because I never had anyone make so much of a fuss over me. Other than that life was going well.

When I went into labor, Ryan was at work about fifteen minutes away from home. I called his job and left an emergency message for his boss. My back was also aching really badly and I could not get comfortable. Ryan got home in less than an 30 minutes from the time that I called him. He bundled up Jamiria and rushed us both to the car. We dropped the Jamiria off at my sister-in-laws house then zoomed off to the hospital.

My pains were coming every two minutes and were very intense. My water had not broken and I was sure I would not have the baby in the car. However, I still wanted to hurry and get to the hospital because I was in so much pain. We already knew that the baby was a boy due to the ultrasound and as far as we knew he was a healthy baby. Once we made it to the hospital, I was placed in a room and given an epidural. I was finally given a chance to relax. Ryan remained with me the whole time and was very attentive but he was very nervous.

Ryan didn't get the chance to see his first son being born, so this was a first time experience for him. I remained in labor for about five hours before it was time to deliver. I was numb from the waist down and thought this was going to be an easy delivery. It wasn't.

When the doctor told me to push, I obeyed, but every time I pushed I felt this sharp pain in my side. It felt like something was caught in my rib cage. Don't ask me how that could be since I had an epidural. The nurses and the doctor thought I was delirious too for a moment. The more they told me to push, I tried but the baby wasn't moving down; and I still had this pain in my side. I broke out in a cold sweat and started to panic because I could feel something wasn't right. It seemed the epidural had worn off and all my efforts to deliver this baby were failing. I was tired; Ryan was looking like he was scared to death which was getting on my nerves. So I screamed for him to get out, but he wouldn't leave. The regular, legs spread eagle and pushing was not working. So they had me turn on my side while they held one leg up and had me push. No progress and the pains were still there. I started screaming, *"Just do a C-Section, I can't do this anymore!"* I was serious as a heart attack I was not pushing anymore, I couldn't handle the pain. The nurse screamed back, "You *have to push because there is no time to do a C-Section, now push and push now!"* I always heard that being in labor was being close to death and during that moment I believed it. I felt I was going to die, I had a baby stuck in me and something felt like it was pulling my ribs apart when I pushed.

However, from somewhere deep within I gathered enough strength and pushed as hard as I could. I was screaming and pushing at the same time. I nearly passed out but within seconds, I heard my baby crying! 8lbs, 9oz maybe that was why I had such a hard time because neither of my other two babies weighed as much. Nonetheless, he was here and I was exhausted! Ryan made it through the delivery and went to call our families and let them know the news. Raphael Princeton Sheffield was taken to the nursery and I was stitched up and taken to a room. Yeah, I know giving the baby part of his father's name was a little risky but I wanted him to have a part of his father. He would never know Princeton as his father because Ryan had proven to be a man of his word so far.

Raphael was such a cute and chunky baby and I loved him already even though he had given his momma such a hard time. Ryan and his family had taken to him also. I was moved with emotion as I watched them bond with him. All was well, but you know it never lasted long in my life. Something was always bound to happen and it did. The next morning the nurse came in the room with some disturbing news. She told me that there was blood in Raphael's stool and she was waiting on the doctor to further examine the baby to find out the cause.

She told me blood being in the stool was not normal but not to worry they were going to do the best for my baby. I didn't panic because she didn't seem alarmed and because she said not too. All that changed about two hours later.

The doctor came in the room and told me that Raphael had a hole in his intestines and that he had to do surgery to repair the hole. That's when my heart dropped, surgery on a newborn baby; I didn't have a good feeling about that. The other thing was that they were transferring my baby to a hospital in Ozark to do the surgery, keep in mind that the hospital in Troy was a small county hospital with few specialties. The hospitals in Ozark were larger and were equipped to handle broader medical cases. I immediately called my mom, she had a way of calming me down and I knew she was a praying woman. Mom immediately noticed the panic in my voice and asked what was wrong. I told her the details that the doctor had shared with me. I didn't know what to do, I was a basket case.

It was a waiting game; I had to wait on the doctor to notify me of Raphael's status. Mom went into prayer over the phone with me. Something about hearing her pray was soothing to my spirit. Mom told me to be prayerful and that everything would be alright. I sure hoped so, but I was so nervous I couldn't pray so I had to rely on her prayers to get us through this crisis. Ryan, Darissa, and Jocelyn who is Ryan's sister arrived at the hospital together to visit and see the baby. I had to break the news to them that Raphael was being transferred to Ozark Children's hospital. Ryan did his best to comfort me as did everyone else in the room. We waited and tried to remain positive.

About three hours later the phone in my room rang; it was the doctor. He called to deliver an update on the baby. I dropped the phone and burst into tears. I was gasping for breath as I tried to cry out, *"NO, No, no!"* Ryan picked up the phone and listened to the doctor tell him that my baby was going to die! The damage to Raphael's intestines was more serious than the doctor thought. Somehow his intestines did not develop; his intestines were mangled and irreparable. Raphael only had a couple of hours to live. Darissa and everyone tried to console me but I wasn't listening to anything they had to say. I just wanted to go be with my baby. I remember Jocelyn and Darissa helping me get dressed.

My doctor had already been notified of the circumstances and gave the authorization for me to be discharged. I really don't remember the 45minute drive to the hospital my mind was in a frenzy. I remember thinking this is surreal, I must be dreaming, this can't be happening. I kept hoping I would wake up and realize I'd had a bad nightmare. When we arrived at the hospital and I was taken to the NICU where Raphael was, I realized it was not a dream. Seeing my beautiful little bundle of joy lying there helpless, reminded me of when Mynesha was born. Mynesha made it through but her little brother was not going to be so fortunate. Raphael had a tiny IV in his foot. The nurse said it was easier to find the vein there than in his hand. He was also hooked up to another monitor that was monitoring his heart rate. The machine was constantly beeping and the nurse explained that his heart rate was dropping. Here I was holding this baby that I had only known for a brief moment but my heart was breaking knowing that I wouldn't get the chance to see him take his first baby step. I wouldn't be able to take pictures of him in all the cute outfits we'd bought for him. I was praying that he would detect that his mommy was holding him and somehow he would gain strength to fight. I whispered to him, *"Mommy is here now,"* as I continuously kissed him on the cheeks. "Beep, Beep," the monitor rang again.

I looked up at the monitor numbers and it was on 40. I knew enough to understand that once the numbers hit zero that his heart had stopped. Raphael was medicated so he was not in any pain. The nurse said it would be a peaceful transition. Peaceful for him, but not for me! I was being tormented having to sit here and watch my baby die and I couldn't do anything about it.

Ryan was there beside me but there was nothing he could do or say that would make this emotional pain go away. My mind thought of Princeton as I rocked our baby in my arms. I wondered what he would say or do if he knew his child was dying. It was irrelevant because Princeton didn't even know he had a son. My mind thought of many things as I continued to rock my baby; life is so precious. It's one thing to give birth and to watch a life come into this world. But it is something unexplainable about watching someone die. So many unanswered questions, why? Where did their spirit go that quickly? What are they feeling? Questions that no one can answer because it's not like we can step into death and step back out and tell of the experience. Once you enter into death there is no coming back. It's a sure thing.

Suddenly, while singing to my baby and gently rocking him in my arms, the *'beep beep'* turned into BeeeeeeeP..........BeeeeeeP. It was a continuous loud sound. I looked up and the numbers had fallen to zero. The nurses came rushing over and told me that he was gone. She said it so softly and tenderly but as if it was normal. She took the baby from me and I ran out of the room screaming and hollering, when I reached the hallway, Ryan's mother was standing there and I fell into her arms bawling! Screaming and hollering with everything in me, from my guts, I cried, *WHhhhyy, Whhhyy?"*

A myriad of questions crowded my mind. I didn't understand why he would take my innocent baby. Was I being punished for the wrong I had done in my life? Was this God's way of getting back at me? Why was my life always filled with misery. Why didn't my mom's prayer work this time as it had done many times before? Why, why, why? Nobody could answer my questions. Nobody. Ryan and I were allowed to have a few moments with Raphael after they had taken all the tubes out of him. He looked as if he was sleeping but I knew he would never

ever wake up again. We didn't have any life insurance on the baby; therefore we had to make a decision as to what to do with the baby. I had no clue. We didn't have any money to properly bury him. One of the staff at the hospital told us that they could dispose of the baby. At that moment it seemed the only thing to do. Sometimes now I think I made a cruel decision to let my baby be burned in a hospital incinerator. I learned from that experience never to make emotional decisions. I just wish I had learned it months earlier.

Going home without a baby felt weird, you leave going to the hospital with the intentions of bringing home a child but that doesn't happen. I came home with a prescription of Xanex to help calm my nerves. Getting over the loss of a baby was rough but thank goodness I had a strong support system. Ryan's parents and family were of a great support for me, being that my parents lived back in Georgia. Darissa was around too but we never saw each other that much after I got married. Of course my other older siblings lived out of state. I poured all my attention into Jamiria.

Ryan, Jamiria and I continued life as a family. However, Ryan's constant jealousy progressed and was driving me crazy. You would think life would be gravy since Ryan had accepted the call to preach. Everyone was happy and elated of the fact that he was becoming a preacher; except for me. I knew the real truth of the chaos that was happening with in our home. But who was I to question what God ordains? After losing Raphael, Ryan and I decided to really get involved in church. Church was the one place that I could get release from the pressures of life. Sometimes I wished I could stay at church all day, seven days a week; because once I left church I would have to deal with the hell I sometimes secretly lived in. From the outside looking in we appeared to be the perfect little couple but on the inside looking out, I was silently crying for help but no one saw me.

Ryan and I later had two kids of our own. Prior to our twin daughters La'nyse and Ja'nyse being born, I became pregnant three months after Raphael died. I delivered another baby boy. You wouldn't think that tragedy would strike twice but it did. Three months after, Ryan Jr. was born I found him cold and clammy in his crib. Dead. Crib death was the cause of death. I can't tell you how traumatic it is to find your baby dead.

I'm not even going to relive the events of that day but just know I was angry at God for a long time. I didn't understand. Why would God grant my request to have a baby boy, grant the request; then take him? Not once but twice he takes the one thing that I had fervently prayed for. Just when I was beginning to have a deeper faith in God he rocked my world in the worse way by taking another innocent child. This difficult time in my life, caused me to be thrown into a cycle of depression.

I was still going to church, singing in the choir, assisting in different ministries but I was depressed. Guess what the saddest part of if it all was; no one noticed. No one in the church or at my job ever noticed that I was suffering from depression and if they did they never said anything. I was always in the midst of the saints, preachers and sometimes prophets and prophetess but no one ever singled me out. After all the prayer lines, healing and deliverance services; I still went home silently suffering. Not just because of the deaths of my babies but the because of everything else going on in my life.

Ryan's jealous rage was driving me insane! He was constantly accusing me of cheating on him. Anytime, I went anywhere without him I was interrogated about who I talked to and what we talked about. I would always have to give a time as to how long I would be gone any time I left home. If I went to the store and said I'd be back in an hour, I'd better be back in 59 minutes or else. One minute later than the time I said would spark curiosity. *"I thought you said you would be back in an hour, it took you an hour and fifteen minutes! What were you doing, he would quiz?"* Therefore, I'd have to give him a detailed account of what happened at the store. I remember one time he watched me leave the house as I was headed to pick Mynesha up from school.

There were two ways that I could go from our house. Normally, I went left out of our drive way but this day I decided for no particular reason to go right. When we walked back in the house he pushed me into the corner screaming and yelling who did I meet at the bottom of the hill? It took me almost an hour to get him off my back. I thought I had left this mess and misery when I divorced Michael, but seemingly I still had to deal with the same mess.

Nothing I did to reassure him that I loved him and wanted to be with him made him feel secure. We went and talked with the pastor at our church and he tried to counsel us but Ryan would only point the blame at me. Mind you I was an extrovert and talked to everyone; I was drawn to people and people were drawn to me. I do admit that on occasion I would flirt but it was nothing serious and I never did it in front of Ryan.

Ryan on the other hand was more of an introvert. He didn't have many friends outside the church. And when he wasn't at the church or working he was mostly at home. I decided I wanted to go to school for cosmetology. I had received my GED and wanted to do something for me, other than being a baby making machine. Ryan agreed at first but soon me going to school became a problem. He honestly felt that I was going to get my degree, get a better job and leave him.

I knew then that he had a major insecurity problem. His jealousy showed no discrimination, I've been accused of sixteen year old boys in our youth church group and every man in between to the sixty year old deacon. All this craziness was taking place as he was the Assistant Pastor at our church. Sometimes we argued and fussed all the way from home to the church parking lot. However, Ryan would get to church and have everybody shouting and speaking in tongues. I would sit there in disbelief. My emotions always showed on my face. I didn't know how to hide them. I couldn't play with God, I'm not saying he was but I knew I wasn't feeling what everyone else was feeling.

When one is constantly being ridiculed and accused of cheating and you know you are not, it pushes you to the edge. *"One day you are going to accuse me of cheating and it's going to be true,* I spat at Ryan during a heated argument. Honestly, at that moment I had no intentions of cheating on Ryan but I wanted to hurt him like he had been hurting me. I felt like I was living in a prison. I used to hate coming home because I had gotten to the point where I didn't want to be around Ryan. I didn't know how to turn this disastrous situation around. I found solace at work around the drug and alcohol addicts I worked with. I was supposed to be the stronger person and help them in their time of weakness; little did they know they were also helping me by taking my mind off the craziness of my life.

Once Ryan came to my job and acted a plum fool. He did a surprise visit and found me playing pool with one of the residents. He asked to see me in the hallway and commenced to accusing me of going with this drug addicted guy. Seriously? How dare he think that I would do something like that! He gave me so much flack about working there that I ended up quitting to appease him. I later got a job at a Mental retardation residential facility.

Most times there were always two people working one shift with the exception of the overnight shift. The rule at the facility was that we were not supposed to leave until our shift was over. However, on occasion we would leave to go get something to eat, especially if we didn't want what was on menu at the job. It just so happens I left to go to McDonalds and the other staff member covered for me until I got back.

While I was gone Ryan happens to call, my co-worker advised him that I had stepped out for a moment. When I got back to the job, food in tow, he told me Ryan had called. I already knew it was about to be some drama, I just didn't know how much.

Ryan was calling from work and I was working as the overnight person that night. My co-worker shift ended at six o'clock, so I was there alone with my MMR residents. I was waiting on Ryan to call me back so I could explain but he never did. I knew he had to pick the kids up after he got off from work so I planned to call him once I thought he was home. At about eight o'clock there was a knock at the door when I opened the door standing behind the screen door was Ryan.

Glaring at me were a pair of fiery red eyes, he looked demonic almost. "He told me to come outside, I didn't want to open the door but I knew if I didn't he was going to cause a ruckus. I didn't want him to alarm my patients so I did. I looked towards the car and was able to see the kids in the car, so I felt maybe he wouldn't act a fool with them around.

Wrong move; As soon as I opened the door he grabbed my arm and yanked me down the steps and body slammed me to the ground. I jumped up as fast as I could, but my arm felt like it was broken. As he was coming towards me again he yelled, *"I'm going to kill you, Where were you?"* He yanked that same left arm and swung me towards the brick wall. My head hit the wall. As he was pinning me to the wall, I could hear Jamiria screaming*," Daddy NO! Stop Daddy Stop!"*

We both looked towards the car at the same time to see Jamiria hanging out the window screaming with fear in her eyes. She saved my life because I just knew he was going to kill me, the anger in his eyes told me so. He let go of me and hopped in the car and left. I ran in the house and called my manager and told her I had an emergency and needed coverage for the evening. Once she arrived, I headed to the hospital but not before calling our Pastor and telling him that I was going to have my husband arrested! I was furious! I had had enough! I was not going to live this life of abuse again.

Pastor Grant begged me not to call the police and to let him deal with it. I guess he was more concerned about the image of the church than he was about me. I agreed not to press charges but I was not going home with him. When I reached the hospital, Pastor Grant and Ryan were waiting for me. As I walked past them I stated, *"Please keep him away from me or else he will be in jail tonight!"* I guess Pastor Grant knew I was serious and he made Ryan wait in the waiting room. He asked me if I wanted him to stay with me and I told him No and that I would be ok.

My arm was sprung and I had a few other lumps and bruises. Thank goodness that was all that was wrong. Before leaving the hospital I called Jacoby to let him know I needed a place to stay for the night. He happily obliged me. I explained to Jacoby in minimum detail about what happened because I didn't need him in my business or too give him false hope that we could get back together. Jacoby and I maintained a relationship because of Jamiria and he made it quite clear that he wanted me back. It wasn't happening but I made sure to keep a good relationship with him to ensure Jamiria didn't go lacking for anything. Ryan was a good provider but sometimes when things got tight I called on Jacoby and he would always help me out. That's a little tad-bit of info that Ryan didn't need to know.

No, I didn't leave Ryan after that incident but I made his life hell for a few weeks. He begged my forgiveness and for a few months things were going well. However, I knew it was just a matter of time before he had his flare up. It's how we functioned. We lived a roller coaster life. Pastor Grant kept things hush-hush from the church and Ryan continued on preaching and working in the church as if nothing had ever happened.

Sure enough as I knew it would, Ryan started back with his jealous antics. One Sunday after church he saw me talking to one of the married deacons of the church. We were standing dead in the middle of the church, surrounded by other members talking about an upcoming program. When we got home he tried to choke the life out of me because he felt I was smiling at the man the wrong way. Again, I saw my life flash before my eyes as he had his hands around my throat. I tried to scream, but nothing would come out. I felt the blood rushing from my brain as his grip tightened. I don't know what caused him to let go, but he did. And when he did, my limp body fell to the floor.

I felt my throat contracting from the release of his strong hold. It took a moment before I could gather my bearings. But when I did I gathered my kids and went to a hotel. Brundidge isn't that big so it only took Ryan driving around to all the few decent hotels in the city to find me. Again, he begged me to come home and he apologized. I had no choice but to go back because I didn't make enough money to take care of me and the kids. The church also played a major part in the reason I stayed as long as I did. Every time Ryan and I would mention divorce, Pastor Grant would mention how the church would be affected and how many people looked up to us.

Divorce would affect both our ministries. I had been licensed as a missionary, which is what they called female ministers at my church; and of course Ryan was the Assistant Pastor. Therefore, I held on a little while longer for the sake of others. I loved Ryan but I was quickly starting to resent him for all the hell he was putting me through. Emotionally, I was a wreck.

Things got worse between us in a way that I didn't see coming. One week my parents came up to visit on vacation and we were all watching the Oprah show. I will never forget this day. Oprah was interviewing a father and his family. The man had been accused of molesting all three of his daughters. The mother claimed she didn't know but the daughters claimed she did but didn't do anything about it. Of course the father claimed he didn't do it. It was a very emotional and heated show. I was ok with watching it until my father said and I quote,*" I don't know what would make a man do such a thing to his daughters!"* Something about hearing those words opened the floodgates of my memory.

Everything that my dad ever did to me came rushing into my mind. Understand up until this point I had not told anyone what had happened to me, not even Ryan. It took everything within me to not tell everyone in the room. But I had my mom to protect, plus I was a grown woman, what good would it do to tell now. So I bottled it up and ignored my father's comments.

That night when Ryan was trying to get his groove on, I clammed up. I didn't want to be bothered because I had slipped into one of my moments. I just wanted to be left alone with my thoughts. But Ryan wouldn't take no for an answer. He just kept at me to give in.

It seemed the more he was rubbing and tugging at me the more he reminded me of my dad. He finally climbed on me and starting kissing my neck with no regard to my reactions. It was all about him. When he did that I burst into tears and yelled at him to get off me. You would have thought he was raping me; in my mind he was. I was yelling all kind of things at him as I pushed him off of me. *"You just like my dad, but I'm not doing it anymore. I'm not doing it anymore, I yelled!"* I jumped out the bed and was staring at Ryan still screaming and crying.

Ryan came over and grabbed me and asked what I was talking about. The cat was out the bag so I told him the history with my dad and how he had molested me all those years. I was looking for comfort and reassurance but what I got was incomprehension. Ryan failed to connect with me that night. He didn't understand the effect that molestation had on me. Instead he simply said, *"I am sorry that happened to you, but that was then and this is now. I am not your father, I am your husband."* And he proceeded to manipulate me into having sex with him. I gave in to him and let him have his fulfillment. He didn't care that I was not involved in the act, he didn't seem to notice the tears wetting my pillow, and he didn't hear the pain in my voice as I shared my detriment. He didn't care, it was all about him. Who was going to care about me?

I don't think I ever looked at Ryan the same after that incident. I became emotionally detached from him. I rarely wanted him to touch me in any sexual way, because every time he did for some reason reminded me of the abuse of my father. I felt forced to perform. Of course Ryan was still accusing me of every Dick, Tom and Harry; the fact that I was now pulling away from him added to the fire. I wasn't thinking of any man but his continuous accusations and the lack of emotional support were pushing me further away from him. He was pushing me into the arms of someone else.

I had a brief affair with my first love in Georgia. I didn't plan it but it happened. I went to visit my parents one day after an argument with Ryan. I hopped in the car and hit the highway to blow off some steam and I just kept driving. About five hours later I was in Lafayette, Georgia. Mom was glad to see me and so was Mynesha who was six years old now. I hadn't been home in Georgia in about two years. I was happy to be back and to see everybody.

That same night I was hanging with my old friend Honey at the club. I knew everybody congregated at that one place and I was bound to see all my old friends there. As we were sitting there reminiscing about old times, in walked Tyler Davis. Our eyes immediately locked. I hadn't seen Tyler since I moved from Lafayette years ago. Whenever I went home to visit I didn't see him because he was still in the Army. Almost ten years later and he is staring me in the face. He sauntered over and gave me the biggest hug! I was happy to see him as he was to see me. He joined Honey and I at the table and we began to catch up on old times.

While I was sitting there catching up with them, I couldn't help but think what Ryan was thinking. I knew he was probably having a conniption fit because he didn't know where I was. But I was sure he had called mom and dad by now. I really didn't care because I needed time to clear my head. Tyler asked me how long I was going to be in town and I told him just a day or two. He wasted no time with asking me could he take me to lunch the next day and I hastily agreed. I instantly knew it was the wrong thing to do but I couldn't help myself; I wanted to spend some time with him.

We met up and went to Western Sizzling the next day. He caught me up on all the old friends that used to live in the neighborhood and what was going on with him. He hadn't married yet but was back with his high school girlfriend. Tyler was flirting with me and was full of compliments. I was eating them up like I was starving. Truth was I was starving for attention. I had heard nothing but derogatory things from Ryan; he rarely paid me any compliments. Therefore, I welcomed the attention I was receiving from Tyler. After lunch we went and walked around the park and enjoyed the scenery. It was a very refreshing day. Tyler apologized for what happened when I was younger. He admitted that he was wrong for how he treated me. I wasn't expecting an apology but I accepted it. After the park we drove back to his apartment in town. I was enjoying every moment of our time together even though I knew it was short lived.

I couldn't help but wish that Ryan was as attentive as Tyler was being at this very moment. Yes, he did ask me about Ryan and I admitted we were having problems and that I didn't want to talk about it with him; and we didn't. Once we arrived back at Tyler's place we went inside. I promised myself I was only going to stay for a few moments. It didn't happen. It was like we both were thinking the same thing because once we crossed the threshold we were in each other's arms kissing!

I completely allowed myself to forget I was married and that I was the wife of an assistant Pastor. For a brief moment, I didn't care that I was the youth minister at my church. All of my worries, stress and concerns went out the window as I was engulfed in Tyler's love. Sad to say, I enjoyed every moment. It was wonderful and satisfying and at that moment I had no regrets.

Before, I left Georgia I talked to Ryan and let him know I was on the way home. Like always he was apologetic and said we would work things out. He agreed to go to counseling or whatever it took to make our marriage work. The conversation made me feel really bad about what I had done but there was no way to retract it. I just needed to figure out how to correct it.

As I was traveling back home that same day of my indiscretion, guilt set in. My mind took me back to all the many times that Ryan had come to my rescue. He was there for me when I didn't have any where to go. He stood by me when I was pregnant with another man's baby. He comforted me after the deaths of our children.

He did provide for our family. I was indebted to him but look how I was repaying him; by having a one night stand. I knew I couldn't live with myself. Ryan always in his anger called me a *'no good cheat',* this time he would be right.

Once I got home, I was glad to see the kids and Ryan welcomed me with open arms. I couldn't look him in the face, I was afraid he would see the guilt on my face. He didn't accuse me of anything or ask what I had been doing while I was gone. Most times he didn't interrogate me when I would leave for a day or two because he knew he was the reason I would leave.

I didn't tell Ryan what happened out of fear. Who knows what he would have done. Punch holes in the walls and turn over tables like he had done many times before? Or would he try to choke the life out of me; he had tried that before too? Maybe he would try to kill us all like he had threatened to do before I left going to Georgia. Me and my crazy self didn't think about none of that while I was laid up in Tyler's arms.

Funny, how when you are caught up in your sins, the devil doesn't show you the repercussions of your sins. It's not until after the sin has been committed that you remember what is at stake. God is constantly talking to you and lovingly telling you not to do it; walk away. But we override that still small voice. Maybe God needs to start yelling at us; because that small quiet voice telling me not to go in Tyler's apartment didn't work. But I can clearly hear the devil telling me that Ryan is going to Kill Me when he finds out, but he didn't say that before I got caught up. Now I know how Adam and Eve felt.

Ryan found out about my affair by being nosey and insecure. I wrote a letter to my mother explaining the details of the events while I was in town and was asking her for advice. I had the letter in the stamped envelope and addressed to my mother. It was on the dresser waiting to be mailed the next morning. Saturday mornings, we all usually sleep in late. Ryan had to go to the church that morning for a meeting.

He asked me did I want him to mail the letter for me. In my grogginess, I said yes and went back to sleep. The next thing I know I'm awakened by his yelling," *I knew you were a slut, how dare you cheat on me, you ain't about nothing!"* I sat straight up in the bed and told him to quit yelling before he wakes the kids up. *"I don't care about waking up the kids; they need to know their momma is a tramp!"* He was letting it rip! I was scared and mad at the same time. I was scared because I didn't know what he was going to do but I was mad because he read my mail! A letter addressed to my mother; how dare he open my letter written to my mother! Surprisingly, he was mad but not as angry as I thought he would be. He swung on me but I dodged the blow. He threw the letter down and left. All I could muster out was I'm sorry as he walked out the bedroom. Sorry that I had given him the upper hand and proven him right. I was guilty as sin.

An hour after Ryan left the house, Pastor Grant called. Ryan had told him about what I had done. I was mad and humiliated and now it was time to face the music. Pastor Grant asked me to come to the church so we could talk about it. I told him I didn't want to talk about it, the damage had been done. If Ryan wanted to leave he could leave. I didn't want to keep talking about it. I knew if Ryan stayed he was going to keep throwing it up in my face. I actually felt relieved that he had found out. Pastor Grant didn't put up much of an argument and said he would see me at church the next day.

I ended up going to church but wished I had stayed at home. It seemed everybody was staring at me with disdain. In a small church it doesn't take long for word to spread. Not only did I have to ask Ryan for forgiveness I had to ask God for forgiveness. Pastor sat me down for a few weeks until the storm blew over. That was even more humiliating being at church and not being able to participate and having people talk about you; but I made it thru. Some people showed support but others walked past me as if I were the plague. Not to mention Ryan made me feel like the scum of the earth.

Life at home didn't get better, Ryan and I was at each other's throat all the time. I wished he had just left rather than to stay and make my life a living hell. I hated him! He accused me of still cheating on him but that was not true. The stress became so overwhelming that I felt the only way to get out of it were to die.

One night I took an overdose of Tylenol. I poured a bunch of pills in my hand and rinsed them down with water. I went to bed and waited to die. Ryan and the kids had no clue what I had done. I loved my babies but I didn't want them to continue seeing me in this mess that I was in. Nor did I want them to continue living in a hostile environment. Maybe if I were gone things would change for them. I knew if I were dead things would change for me because I would no longer be living in this hell.

I knew suicide was a sin and I would go to hell for killing myself. But when you are already living in hell , you feel it couldn't be any worse than the hell you are already in. Deep down I didn't want to die, I just wanted this pain that I was feeling to go away. Pain that no one knew I had. The silent pain that I couldn't put my hands on, I was hurting inside and I couldn't even explain it. I'd rather have the bruises of physical pain because at least I can doctor on the bandages. But emotional pain is harder to heal and I didn't know where to begin. It was like I knew I was sick but I couldn't explain the symptoms.

God must have had his hands on me. Instead of dying I woke up vomiting uncontrollably. Ryan took me to the emergency room. I lied and told them that I had had a bad migraine and was popping Tylenols every hour. The doctor believed me and gave me a prescription for nausea and sent me home. Though I was glad I didn't die, I was still hoping that maybe the doctor would see through my lie and recognize I was depressed. He didn't. So I kept functioning as best I could in my dysfunction. I kept living this never-ending lie; putting on a front for the people. I gave true meaning to the term, *'the walking dead.'*

Rumor had been circulating that Ryan was messing around with a girl from his job. When I asked him about it he adamantly denied it and I believed him. I knew he would never cheat on me because he had been so dogmatic about me cheating on him. I felt he would never cheat on me because he was always throwing up in my face about cheating and how he was committed to his marriage. However, the person that was spreading the rumors of his infidelities wouldn't let up.

She kept telling people that he was different at work than he was at church. It became such an issue that even Pastor Grant called us into his office to discuss the issue. Ryan denied every allegation. Maybe she wanted my husband. I couldn't figure it out. I didn't have any signs that Ryan was cheating on me. For the most part he was at work, church and home making my life a living hell.

Instead of life getting better it got worse. I felt that I was about to lose my mind. I was tired of the arguing and making up. I was tired of having to explain and prove myself. Two years had passed since my indiscretion but you would have thought it was yesterday because of how Ryan kept reminding me about it. When he thought I was too happy he would find a way to ruin my happiness. He told me one day, I didn't deserve to be happy after what I had done. Maybe he was right.

One day, I decided I was leaving, I was fed up. I didn't have a *'last nerve'* left for anyone to get on. I will never forget this day because it is the day that I knew God loved me and that he was truly real. I called my mom and told her that I was coming home. By this time my parents had moved back to Alabama due to my mom's illness. Alabama had better doctors. Anyway, she didn't say a whole lot when I told her I was coming home, she simply said, *"Well if that's what you feel you have to do, do it. And I'll let your dad know."* That was all I needed to hear.

After hanging up the phone, I fell back on the bed and cried like a baby. I was so overwhelmed with grief. As I was crying my heart out, I began to pray to God. *"God, I know you don't authorize divorce and I know you have all Power in your hands. You have the power to fix this marriage. Whether you choose to dissolve it or whether you choose to fix it. I don't care how you do it but just grant me peace. Grant me Peace in however you decide to fix it."* As soon as I finished my prayer, I kept hearing Psalms 37, Psalms 37. I finally picked up my Bible and read Psalms 37 in its entirety.

Psalms 37:1-40

1 *Do not fret because of those who are evil*
or be envious of those who do wrong;
2 *for like the grass they will soon wither,*
like green plants they will soon die away.
3 *Trust in the LORD and do good;*
dwell in the land and enjoy safe pasture.
4 *Take delight in the LORD,*
and he will give you the desires of your heart.
5 *Commit your way to the LORD;*
trust in him and he will do this:

[6] He will make your righteous reward shine like the dawn,
your vindication like the noonday sun.
[7] Be still before the LORD
and wait patiently for him;
do not fret when people succeed in their ways,
when they carry out their wicked schemes.
[8] Refrain from anger and turn from wrath;
do not fret—it leads only to evil.
[9] For those who are evil will be destroyed,
but those who hope in the LORD will inherit the land.
[10] A little while, and the wicked will be no more;
though you look for them, they will not be found.
[11] But the meek will inherit the land
and enjoy peace and prosperity.
[12] The wicked plot against the righteous
and gnash their teeth at them;
[13] but the Lord laughs at the wicked,
for he knows their day is coming.
[14] The wicked draw the sword
and bend the bow
to bring down the poor and needy,
to slay those whose ways are upright.
[15] But their swords will pierce their own hearts,
and their bows will be broken.
[16] Better the little that the righteous have
than the wealth of many wicked;

17 for the power of the wicked will be broken,
but the LORD upholds the righteous.
18 The blameless spend their days under the LORD's care,
and their inheritance will endure forever.
19 In times of disaster they will not wither;
in days of famine they will enjoy plenty.
20 But the wicked will perish:
Though the LORD's enemies are like the flowers of the field,
they will be consumed, they will go up in smoke.
21 The wicked borrow and do not repay,
but the righteous give generously;
22 those the LORD blesses will inherit the land,
but those he curses will be destroyed.
23 The LORD makes firm the steps
of the one who delights in him;
24 though he may stumble, he will not fall,
for the LORD upholds him with his hand.
25 I was young and now I am old,
yet I have never seen the righteous forsaken
or their children begging bread.
26 They are always generous and lend freely;
their children will be a blessing.[b]
27 Turn from evil and do good;
then you will dwell in the land forever.
28 For the LORD loves the just
and will not forsake his faithful ones.

Wrongdoers will be completely destroyed[c];
the offspring of the wicked will perish.
29 The righteous will inherit the land
and dwell in it forever.
30 The mouths of the righteous utter wisdom,
and their tongues speak what is just.
31 The law of their God is in their hearts;
their feet do not slip.
32 The wicked lie in wait for the righteous,
intent on putting them to death;
33 but the LORD will not leave them in the power of the wicked
or let them be condemned when brought to trial.
34 Hope in the LORD
and keep his way.
He will exalt you to inherit the land;
when the wicked are destroyed, you will see it.
35 I have seen a wicked and ruthless man
flourishing like a luxuriant native tree,
36 but he soon passed away and was no more;
though I looked for him, he could not be found.
37 Consider the blameless, observe the upright;
a future awaits those who seek peace.[d]
38 But all sinners will be destroyed;
there will be no future[e] for the wicked.
39 The salvation of the righteous comes from the LORD;
he is their stronghold in time of trouble.

40 *The LORD helps them and delivers them;*
he delivers them from the wicked and saves them,
because they take refuge in him.

This passage of scripture ministered to my spirit. I felt comfort through the scriptures. The Lord continued to minister to me and in a still small voice, I heard him say, *"Not now, now is not the time to leave. I will deliver you and when I do, there will be nothing anyone can say."* Sometimes when God speaks he doesn't give you all the details. I kept pondering what he meant about *'he was going to deliver me in a way where no one could say anything.'* He never said anything else but I was assured that everything was going to be alright.

I actually called my mom back and told her everything that God had just told me. Again, she was a woman of few words, *"Always obey the word of the Lord."* When Ryan arrived home from work I even shared my experience with him. He too wondered about how God was going to deliver without anyone saying anything. For a few days I continued to think over my divine revelation. I kept saying to God, *"I don't want you to kill him."* I couldn't think of any other way for God to do what he said he was going to do, other than through death. Death didn't have anything to do with God's plan, and I would soon find that out. The real truth was that both Ryan and I wanted to leave. We knew the marriage was not going to last forever. But because of our status in the church neither of us wanted to be responsible for breaking up our family. Therefore, we stayed to see who would be the first to break. He was hoping it would be me and I was hoping it would be him.

How many know that God is a man of his word? One day, during a time when things between Ryan and I seemed to be going well, he tells me he has something he wanted to tell me; A secret. Ryan dropped a bombshell on me that I was not prepared for! Ryan confessed to having an affair. I was just as shocked as you are. At first I thought he was playing but when I looked into his eyes I knew he wasn't. Shockingly, Ryan had had an affair way before I did. He was the one that had been having an affair all along, while he was accusing me.

Apparently, what I stupidly thought to be a lie was indeed the truth. Ryan was cheating on me with a girl from his job. He had actually introduced me to one of the women. One day I went to pick him up from work and he was walking out with this woman. I didn't think anything about it. They walked to the car and he introduced her as a co-worker. She made small talk about how much Ryan talked about his family, etc. Little did I know that I was the butt of the joke; she was stabbing me in the back while smiling in my face.

I was flabbergasted! A wave of emotions ran through me; Hurt, anger, stupidity, embarrassment and everything in between.

This man had caused me to live a life full of distress. He constantly made me feel like the scum of the earth. My self-esteem was compressed. I had endured years of humiliation and ridicule because of his insecurities and jealousy. All along it was a cover up of his guilt and infidelities. My mother used to always say, *'if someone is constantly accusing you of something then they may be covering something up themselves.'* I was just too dumb and naïve to see it.

Outside of the love I had lost for Ryan, I was still looking at him as my savior. A part of me felt like I owed him something. I continued to accept the condescending comments he made towards me because a part of me felt like I deserved it. I felt like such a fool, I'd been played for a fool. He was out here screwing me over all while he was making me feel like I was the sole problem. He was such a hypocrite.

I didn't have to make a decision whether to stay in my marriage. I didn't get that opportunity. Ryan told me about the affair because he wanted out. He moved in with his mistress and I filed for divorce. He left the church and married his new love shortly after our divorce was final. Everybody at the church was in total disbelief. The whole situation was a mess.

My mom reminded me of the day I was initially going to leave Ryan. She said, *"God kept his word, he did just what he said he was going to do."* When I looked at the situation, she was right. There was nothing anyone could say because I didn't leave my husband, Ryan left me. For some reason God had answered my prayer in an uncanny way. I didn't question him why, I just thanked him for the Peace that I now had within. Oh Yes, I was heartbroken but I still had this overwhelming peace. No matter what was going on I knew I was going to be alright.

After my divorce life became a struggle financially because I had the full responsibility of taking care of my children. However, the peace that I had was well worth it. I was free. I started dating again and enjoying life. I had missed out on so much. My spiritual life was a roller coaster. I still had a love for God but now I had a different struggle. Trying to live a saved life and struggling in my flesh. I was used to having a man. And now that I wasn't married, I struggled with doing what was right spiritually.

I was considered an attractive woman and getting a man was never a problem. And now that I was single I was like a kid in a candy store. Needless to say, I often gave into my sexual desires. It wasn't like I was out giving it up to every man that asked for it, but I was easily mislead by men that acted liked they loved me. I still equated sex and love as the same. If I allowed a man to have sex with me, I immediately thought that he loved me. When a man showed me a lot of attention or even said he loved me then sex would follow. Even if he didn't say he loved me, in my mind if we had sex, I believed he eventually would. I didn't know how to separate the two. The same held true when I met Harvey.

When I met Harvey, I fell head over heels for him. He was everything I desired in a man; Handsome, financially stable, catering, honest, and spiritual. Harvey knew the bible better than I did and we often had these great discussions about the word. Along with all the aforementioned attributes, Harvey allowed me to be myself without judgment. He knew I loved God and that I was a genuinely a good person. However, he also knew that I struggled with trying to contain my flesh. I allowed him to bring out a side of me that I had tried hard to hide. The difference between Harvey and I was that I felt guilty as heck about our sexual escapades but he didn't.

Harvey and I were involved on and off again for about three years. I'd be with Harvey and then go to church and kneel at the altar crying out to God to help me. A week later, I'd be back in the bed with Harvey. I couldn't help myself. I tried to resist him but when I thought of how he made me feel, I'd give in again and again. Thus the cycle would keep repeating itself. Commit a sin and ask for forgiveness; Ask for forgiveness and commit sins. It was the story of my life and the ending would always be the same..............Heartbreak.

MIRACLES

I would like to write that Harvey and I fell madly in love and eventually got married, but that is not the case. I would even like to say that I met another man who was the man of my dreams and we fell in love and lived happily ever after but that isn't true either. The truth is that after Harvey, I continued in a cycle of dead end relationships. Harvey and I broke up in stages. He had developed a pattern with me. The pattern started to change and I knew something was wrong.

He normally would call me several times during the week even if we didn't see each other. I noticed that the calls slowly reduced down to once a week; from once a week to twice a month. His visits were sporadic of course they changed with the phone calls. When I began to question him about the relationship he would say that he was extra busy. He eventually took over his mother's business in Georgia so that took away more time.

I knew I was losing him and there was nothing I could do. I started preparing myself for the day that I would no longer hear from him. When I would try calling him sometimes he wouldn't answer or when he did the conversation was short and vague. It didn't take long for me to figure out there was someone else; but of course he denied it. I finally got tired of holding on to false hope and vowed not to call him unless he called me. It took some time but I eventually conditioned myself to forget about him. The few times he did call, I acted as nonchalant as he did. I missed him terribly and it took a long time for me to get over him, but eventually I did.

Somehow I kept running into the same old type of guy. The charming, handsome, make me laugh and want to have sex with no commitment type guy. Or I'd meet the desperate, overly aggressive, boring, wanna' get married type guy. It seemed I could never meet the perfect guy for me. Going thru all these relationships was emotionally draining. Thank goodness I had sense enough not to become sexually involved with all of them but even still I was emotionally bankrupt. The strange part about it all was that ninety percent of the guys I met and dated were some decent guys. They had decent jobs, their own homes and cars, and not to mention church going men. It wasn't like I was going down to the homeless shelter and picking up men that I had to fix up. Maybe I should have done that because it seems to have worked for a few women I knew. However, I did realize that most men I dealt with did have some type of issue that I felt that I could change or make better by loving them. It never worked.

I was continuously praying and seeking God to bless me with a husband. I tried every relationship formula, read many man grabbing books and said every affirmation known to man and nothing worked. *"He'll come when you get to the point where you don't need a man," one woman told me.* I guess that was how she got her man. Well how do you get to that point? I didn't need a man financially because God continues to bless me beyond measure. However, that didn't take away that I needed and wanted a man for emotional support, love, and physical and sexual gratification. Truth is God designed us to want and need the opposite sex. Another nerve wracking quote, *"Maybe it is not God's will for you to be married,"* some would sincerely say. I totally refused to believe that lie. I feel if God didn't want me to marry then he would take the desire away and since he hadn't, I'd just keep on believing.

I finally got to a point where I was becoming bitter. Even with all my issues, I knew I was a good person and could make someone a great wife. However, it seemed that a good woman is not what men wanted these days. I was becoming bitter and began to question my faith in God. Especially, when I would see many people I knew getting married out of the clear blue. I began to question why was it that God kept allowing me to continue in this cycle of hurt and pain; one person after the other chiseling away at my heart.

It seemed that God was answering every prayer except for the one that I so desperately wanted him to answer. He just had turned a deaf ear to my desires. Didn't he see my heart? Didn't he see that I wanted to do what was right? Was it that hard for him to give me the love that I yearned for? After all, God is love.

The more frustrated I became with my circumstances and with God, the more the devil worked on my mind. *"Maybe, it's ok for you to indulge in a little sin every so often, obviously God hasn't answered your prayers. He understands we are not perfect; that's what Grace and Mercy is for. He forgives all sins."* I was slowly giving into the negative thoughts that were invading my mind. My mind was saying one thing and my heart was saying another. I didn't know which one was going to win.

One night after the break up with another man that I believed to be my soul mate, I had a heart to heart talk with God. Almost everything about this relationship was perfect. This man was very spiritual, had a love for God, he was catering and attentive and affectionate. He believed in family, we had awesome chemistry, great conversations and more. With the exception of a couple of bad habits he was perfect because I was willing to overlook the bad habits. So what was the problem? Timing. He had recently broken up with his girlfriend when our paths crossed. Things between us quickly ignited and I was in heaven; that is until he decided he needed time to sort out his feelings for her. *"Are you serious? God not again! Please don't let this be happening to me again."* I silently cried as I listened to him break the news to me. Heartbreak and devastation!

I cried myself to sleep; I couldn't believe that this was happening to me again. I finally got myself together some days later; it was then that I began to do some soul searching. I needed answers and I needed the truth. There had to be a reason that this kept happening to me. I was tired and fed up and I couldn't allow my heart to be broken again.

It seemed for a minute that God was mad at me and was not talking to me. But I remained persistent. *"God, I know I have not been the perfect person and I have done many things wrong in your sight, but I need your help! If you don't help me no one can. If you don't deliver then I'll forever be in this place of sin, shame and sorrow. God I want to be pleasing in your sight, I want to do what's right but for some reason, I don't have the power within myself to do what is right. I have desire but my strength is weak.*

If you love me, please answer me and let me know that I am not forsaken," I prayed with all sincerity. I really needed and wanted God to answer me. He did answer in his own timing but he didn't answer how I thought he would. I thought it would come instantly and he would speak clear directions to me. He didn't.

Because I was so caught up with my ex, even though we had broken up; I still found myself back in his bed on a few occasions. I was still praying that God would deliver and that somehow he would change the situation between my ex and I. One evening as I lay in his arms and as he was sleeping; tears came from nowhere. I tried to stop them but the more I wiped tears the more they flowed. Tears are sometimes silent prayers. I was talking to God and the spirit was making intercession. I never uttered a word; I just let the tears flow and do the talking for me. When the tears stopped I was a different person. Later, when I left his house I knew it was truly over between us. I knew that I wanted more and deserved more than what I had settled for.

I continued with my soul searching to find the reason for my actions. I wanted to know why I attracted the same type of men in my life. I once heard a famous comedian say, "If *you keep attracting the same type of no good people into your life then maybe there is something wrong with you." (Clean version of what he said and it was funnier)* Funny but sadly true; I'd have to agree. It's not always the other person; the problem sometimes lies within us. In order to find the problem I had to go back to the beginning.

What happened in my childhood that shaped me into the person that I now am? I'm not a psychologist nor am I an expert of psychology. However, I studied psychology in college and have read enough to know that most issues we have as an adult stem from childhood.

One of the first things I realized about myself was that I feared being abandoned. As a child my biological mother gave me up for adoption. Regardless of the reason for her decision; in my mind she abandoned me. She didn't want me. My mom always tried to reassure me that I was a blessing to her; but most times I felt like a curse. I felt rejected and deep down I never really felt a sense of belonging. I always felt something was missing. How did abandonment issues play a part in my relationships?

Clinginess. Clinginess was a reflection of my own insecurities and fears. I didn't want to be alone or feel abandoned; therefore I accepted and stayed in relationships when I knew they were headed to a dead end. I was constantly worried about being dumped.

Insecurity was the foundation of my clinginess. Insecurity made me constantly want to be around the other person, so I could reassure myself that they were still there and hadn't dumped me. It was a sad shape to be in. We haven't even made it to the fact that I was molested for many years by a parent.

Long story made short. I learned that the trauma I experienced in childhood affected me greatly as an adult. Fear, anxiety, shame, sexual promiscuity are all the effects of sexual abuse as a child. Now that I understood the *'Why of my behavior'*, I could work on the *How and the what*. What actions did I need to take to break the many negative emotional chains that had me bound for so long and how was I going to make it happen.

One of the first things I started to do was to release myself of the guilt I felt of being abused. I used to blame myself for allowing the abuse to continue for so long. However, I now know that I was not to blame; it wasn't my fault. I began to quote positive affirmations to myself. *'I am fearfully and wonderfully made, (psalm 139:14*) *"I am loved because I love me, I choose love, joy and peace instead of anger, sadness and chaos."* I learned how to reprogram my thinking which allowed me to stop sabotaging the great life that God has ordained for me.

I began to love me like no one else. My self-esteem improved immensely. Funny thing about me was I always thought I was beautiful on the outside but I hated who I was on the inside. I used to always say that only a few people loved me beyond my physical beauty; not many took the time to get to know the true essence of who I was. The reality of the matter was that I only loved the outer me therefore no one else could truly love the inner me when I didn't love who I was. Today, no one can beat me loving me; I love me some me!

Throughout my behavior modification I learned the power of forgiveness. Just like I asked God to forgive me for all my wrong doings; I also had to forgive all those that wronged me in my life, including my father. I chose not to harbor feelings of hatred in my heart. I finally was able to tell my mother what dad did to me. It was not easy to do but in order to get past my pain and completely heal I had to release my past. I came to understand that I could not protect anyone but myself and my children.

Therefore, I couldn't continue to protect my mom from all the sins of my father. Initially, dad denied it but my mom wouldn't let up. She kept seeking the truth. He never really admitted it but he did say it didn't all happen like I said it did. It didn't matter to me what he said because I knew the truth and so did he, regardless if he admitted it or not. I actually felt sorry for him because he was sick and didn't even realize it. I believe someone may have violated him in order for him to be the way he is; only God knows the truth about that one. Mom was heartbroken but what could she do? Age, health and finances forced her to stay. Even if she could have left I am not sure she would have. I'm just making sure that I don't ever be in a predicament that I have to solely depend on a man, especially to the point that I have to stay when I really want to leave.

Where is the miracle in all the misery and mess? A miracle is defined as: *a surprising and welcome event that is not explainable by natural or logical laws and is considered to be divine. Or it can be a highly improbable or extraordinary event, development, or accomplishment.*

Though many things in my life I did not welcome, I am surprised by the fact that some of them happened. I can truly look back over my life and say that I have lived through some unexplainable and extraordinary events. Still looking for the miracle? The miracle is that I'm still standing! The miracle is that I didn't die in my misery and mess; I lived to tell my story. And I am sharing it all across the world.

The miracle is that my kids and I survived all the turmoil we experienced after the divorce; which is another story by itself. But I learned that I can make it by myself without the financial help of a man. The girls and I lived in a shelter for about four months after we were evicted from an apartment. The miracle is that I swore my kids to secrecy. They were not to tell their father because I was scared he would try to take them from me. Amazingly, they kept the secret and their fathers never found out until years later. Now you know that is a miracle because most kids can't hold water. I can laugh about it now but back then it was no laughing matter.

My father has never been a person to show much emotion. He has always been a prideful person. He has never told me he was sorry for all the things he took me through but I know he is sorry by his actions. I know most therapists say it is necessary to get the apology from the abuser, especially if you still have contact with them. I didn't find it necessary. I consider it a miracle every time I can tell my dad that I love him and mean it. Not many people can salvage a relationship with their abuser but I did. This also adds to the miraculous works of God. While I will never forget what my dad did to me, I can remember without pain. That's when you know you are completely healed; when the memories of your past aren't pain filled.

I can't forget to mention one small childhood prayer that God answered for me and that was to find my birth parents. One day out of the blue I get a phone call from a private investigator stating she thinks she has found my biological family.

Words can't explain how I felt when I laid eyes on pictures of my family. Two of my sisters had been diligently searching for me and after about two years of their searching the investigator found me. I was in total shock! The day I first heard my birth mothers voice was a highly emotional day. I came to learn that I had four sisters and a brother and a host of nieces and nephews. The day I met them all was like a family reunion. I am still getting to know my biological family and though it's been a slow process I am still thankful for the miracle of answered prayers.

The miracle is found in the fact that there was a purpose for my misery and my mess. I didn't understand it at the time but my life was designed and aligned by God. I never could have made it through all the troubles and storms without God. Many have killed themselves from the pressures of life but here I am still alive and loving life. Even when I tried to take my life, God blocked it! He preserved me! It's not cliché when I say, *"I could have lost my mind; it's more than a song that I sing "There were dangers awaiting me, destruction was sure to be."* It's a testament of my life; it's my miracle! I truly understand

and know that I deserve God's best. I don't and I won't settle for less. God doesn't need my help because he is the perfect Match Maker. He is better than Match.com; he already knows my likes and dislikes; my wants and my needs. Also I came to understand that I had to submit my desires and my will to God. Proverbs 19:21 says, Many *are the plans in a person's heart, but it is the LORD's purpose that prevails.*

It did not matter what my desires were because the Lord's purpose would supersede my desires because he knows what is best for me.

So no, this story doesn't end with me meeting my knight and shining armor; there is no prince riding on a white horse to sweep me off my feet. My happiness isn't tied to a man. I would like everyone to understand that true happiness isn't based on the love of another person but true happiness comes from within. Therefore, my story does have a happy ending because I am happy! I am happy to be alive, happy that God saw fit to keep his hands on me. I'm happy that my life is full of purpose. I am happy to be me. I am happy to live a life of expectancy. I am standing in a door of open miracles. No matter how great or small I am expecting a miracle every day. More than anything I am happy to have made it through my misery and my mess; therein lies the greatest Miracle of all!!

ABOUT THE AUTHOR

Angela E. Stevenson is a Freelance writer, author, motivational speaker and teacher. She is very passionate about helping others develop into their best self and fulfilling their God-given talents. Her latest book was written to encourage those that have experienced any type of abuse, specifically child and domestic violence that they can get out and that life is worth living.

Angela is divorced and the mother of four wonderful sons and currently resides in Atlanta, GA.

Discussion Questions

1. **What is your perception of Yolanda as: a child; teenager; adult?**
2. **Do you think that Yolanda's mother was in denial about the abuse?**
3. **What are your thoughts as to why Yolanda kept running into the same type of men?**
4. **Discuss the proposition by Pastor Shelton to Yolanda.**
5. **Was Yolanda wrong in not telling Princeton about the baby?**
6. **Do you think the effects of abuse will forever haunt Yolanda's life?**
7. **Should Christians seek counsel outside the church?**
8. **Could you relate to any aspect of Yolanda's life?**

Questions from the Author

1. **What are your overall thoughts about the book/story?**
2. **Would you like to read a sequel?**

Please share your comments and thoughts@www.miserymess-miracles.com

Made in the USA
Charleston, SC
04 May 2012